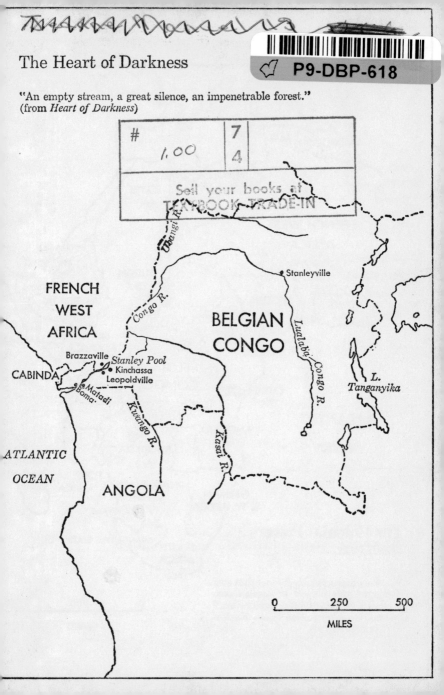

The Heart of Darkness

"An empty stream, a great silence, an impenetrable forest."
(from *Heart of Darkness*)

FRENCH
WEST
AFRICA

CABINDA

Brazzaville
Stanley Pool
Kinchassa
Leopoldville

Matadi
Boma

BELGIAN
CONGO

Stanleyville

Con-go R.

Ubangi

Lualaba

Congo R.

L.
Tanganyika

Kwango R.

Kasai R.

ATLANTIC
OCEAN

ANGOLA

0   250   500
MILES

HEART OF DARKNESS

ALDINE MODERN ENGLISH SERIES

The best expression of what men and women of all nationalities have borne or experienced, have done or have dreamed of doing.

Fiction

Poetry

Other titles in preparation

HEART OF DARKNESS
AN OUTPOST OF PROGRESS
THE LAGOON

JOSEPH CONRAD

With an Introduction, Notes,
and Questions by

ALAN C. COMAN

Head of the Department of English
Victoria Park Secondary School, Toronto

J. M. DENT & SONS (CANADA) LIMITED
TORONTO

Special Canadian School Edition
published by arrangement with
J. M. DENT & SONS LTD. LONDON

CONTENTS

JOSEPH CONRAD

Józef Teodor Konrad Naleçz Korzeniowski was born at Berdiczew, Poland, on December 3rd, 1857. Poland at that time was partitioned among Russia, Prussia, and Austria, and Berdiczew was in Podolia, a Ukrainian province under the Russians. Joseph's childhood was a grim ordeal. His father was arrested by the Russians for his part in the secret meetings of a Polish national movement and was banished to Vologda in northern Russia. On the journey into exile both the boy and his mother fell ill, and, though Joseph recovered, his mother's health was permanently affected, and she died in exile in 1865. The father, to fend off loneliness and isolation, devoted himself to literary projects; but Joseph Conrad's literary career, despite his father's influence, was not to begin until the 1890's.

When his father died at Cracow in 1867, Joseph was put in the care of his uncle. Since the family traditionally pursued careers connected with the land, the army, and the arts, Joseph's announcement in 1872 that he intended to go to sea caused some concern. But he wanted a life that was free from the shadows of the past, and so in 1874 he travelled to Marseilles to begin roving and to realize his dream of adventure. There was no indication at all at this period that he would become one of the most distinguished novelists in the English literary tradition. Yet the extraordinary diversity of his experiences at sea was to provide him with the ships, the men, and the adventures of his novels; with the perceptive understanding of human relationships, dilemmas, hopes, and fears; and with the isolation conducive to the quest for a deep self-knowledge. Many of the novels indeed recapture the essence of his own life's voyage, which was very extensive, for his career at sea took him as far as Australia, the Malay archipelago, the Gulf of Siam, and finally the Congo.

Early in his career as a seaman he was one of a syndicate of gun-runners who bought a sixty-ton 'balancelle', the *Tremolino*, for their trade. Though they spent many nights evading coastguards, customs men, and sentinels, Conrad expressed in a letter written in 1919 that he had found the activities rather unexciting. His interest seems to have centred on the ship they sailed in, and his sensitive affection for her appears in a moving chapter of *The Mirror of the Sea*. Though he did have a brief love affair during this period, and was injured in a duel on account of it, ships were his first love, and more affection is recorded at this time for the *Tremolino* than for any woman. Gun-running and women excited him less than ships, it would seem.

Yet even stronger than his attachment to ships was his fascination for the sea. The sea, Conrad says, gives a man the chance to know himself. But it does more. In *Youth*, the narrator, Marlow, states that 'there are those voyages that seem ordered for the illustration of life, that might stand for a symbol of existence'. Thus the sea gives an insight into both the self and all human society. In *Heart of Darkness* Conrad fuses these two perspectives in a very penetrating examination of both his own true self and the terms of all civilized existence. And here again, the philosophical statement he achieves in this novel is the product of his own experience, for the narrative is drawn from a voyage to the Congo that climaxed Conrad's maritime career. In 1886 he had become a naturalized British subject and had obtained his master mariner's certificate. In 1890, while seeking command of a vessel on the Congo, he made a trip up that river, which, instead of furthering his career, ended it; for the Congo ruined his health and he was forced to abandon the sea altogether. From then on he turned to writing as a career.

In 1896, having settled in England, he married Jessie George, who bore him two sons—Boris, and John Alexander. Adventure now seemed to pursue him, for on one of his occasional trips to the Continent he was caught by the outbreak of war in 1914. He and his family had to escape from Austrian Poland through Austria and Italy to the Mediterranean.

Despite Conrad's lifelong interest in ships, he did not sail on a big liner until 1923, when he visited his publisher in New York. On his return he sought quietude and rest, but his fascination for the sea never left him, and even the day before his death he was working diligently on an article for a volume of sea memories. He died on August 3rd, 1924, and is buried in Canterbury.

Journey – June 1890

Published – 1899

Story
Adventure
Exploitation
Spiritual quest +
Kurtz is Marlow's inspiration
his grail
see self-exercise restraint

INTERPRETING HEART OF DARKNESS

WE often assume that the easiest and best way to know what a novel means is to ask the author where possible for his interpretation of it or to consult any recorded statement of his as a guide to accurate critical appreciation. And certainly the author's own comments are valuable aids to criticism; but, while he best may know what his intentions were, he may be too involved with the work, too near to it to make an accurate objective appraisal. Intention and accomplishment are often very different things, and many an author is undoubtedly amazed to discover the merits and qualities that scholars, critics, and students quite validly point to in his work. Nor by acknowledging that the novelist's art is as often instinctive and spontaneous as it is conscious and deliberate, do we in any way belittle his achievement. Whatever the method, the genius is his alone.

Yet Joseph Conrad did make the following statement about *Heart of Darkness*, which we may use as a springboard to critical evaluation of the novel:

> In the light of the final incident, the whole story in all its descriptive detail shall fall into place—acquire its value and its significance . . . the interview of the man and the girl locks in—as it were—the whole

30,000 words of narrative description into one suggestive view of the whole of life, and makes of that story something quite on another plane than an anecdote of a man who went mad in the Centre of Africa.

(Conrad to Wm. Blackwood, 31st May, 1902, in *Letters to William Blackwood* (N.C.), 1958, p. 154)

He sees the novel as a 'view of the whole of life' no less, and conceives of all the details (presumably of character, point of view, narrator lens, setting, mood, literary association, structure, and thought, etc.) as falling into place and acquiring 'value' and 'significance'. The concluding piece that locks in the other parts of the design and reveals its full 'significance' is Marlow's interview with Kurtz's Intended, the final incident of the novel. Conrad's tone scorns the literal view of the work as 'an anecdote of a man who went mad in the Centre of Africa', and he implies that we should lift this story from the particular to the universal. It is not simply inconsequential fiction to titillate the reader's idle fancy.

But it is still all too easy to assume that the theme is clearly stated if we should only give the proper significance to descriptive detail. And Conrad warns us of this assumption. The meaning of the novel is intentionally unclear. It is like the glow that 'brings out a haze'; it is enveloped in 'misty haloes'. Even at the climax, the experience is shrouded in darkness and uncertainty. The statement of the novel is indeed so inconclusive, so uncertain, that it has led the noted critic F. R. Leavis to observe that Conrad is 'intent on making a virtue out of not knowing what he means'. But if in this novel Marlow, Conrad's narrator, has 'peeped over the edge' and discovered 'the horror' of the truths of existence, he nevertheless sees that they cannot be conveyed in any simple moral truism or

aphorism to people who live, as his listeners and we ourselves do, 'each moored with two good addresses, like a
hulk with two anchors, a butcher round one corner, a
policeman round another, excellent appetites, and temperature normal—normal from year's end to year's end'.
The truths that Marlow discovers are sensed, are felt and
understood rather than said. There is no attempt at
persuasion, since the uninitiated cannot comprehend.
Only the first narrator is affected by the experience of
Marlow's narrative, and he comments scornfully on
Marlow's story before he hears it. The other listeners
seem totally unaffected, and since they do not even
acknowledge the story when it is told, they certainly do
not sense 'the horror' of its truths. They are tempera-
mentally uninitiated in such truths; they, and the people
in Brussels on Marlow's return, and Kurtz's Intended,
live a kind of illusion; they have not the sensibilities to
respond to the wavelengths of Marlow's communication.
His frustration is revealed in the following statement:

> . . . No, it is impossible; it is impossible to convey
> the life-sensation of any given epoch of one's existence
> —that which makes its truth, its meaning—its subtle
> and penetrating essence. It is impossible. We live,
> as we dream—alone . . .

Only the first narrator has the temperament, and Marlow
takes him on a journey into the heart of darkness where he
descends into the 'Inferno' of man's primitive urges—
into the terrifying caverns of man's subconscious. He
glimpses through Marlow's story the 'significance' of life
itself. The question we must now ask is 'Do we?'
It is important to note that there is no one absolutely
true and final view of this work. In fact, this novel perhaps
more than any other of Conrad's has occasioned the

widest possible literary argument, and the disputes are at present far from resolved. It is therefore not my intention as editor to suggest some oversimplified statement of the theme of the novel, but rather to take the student on a systematic study of it, taking account of the descriptive detail as it seems significant or relevant. In the questions at the end of the book, the student is asked to respond to crucial phrases or details and to fit them into a patterned relationship with other significant aspects of the novel. But there is a danger in this approach. The questions have a drift or bias and tend to lead to an ultimate synthesis that coincides with my own view of the novel. The student should therefore be on his guard against being led where he believes he should not go, and he should be ready at all times to challenge the drift of the questions if he believes them to misinterpret or place wrong emphasis upon the particular area of study. We are not dealing with absolutes, but with relative degrees of probability.

Since I began by quoting what the author said about his novel, let me end by quoting him again, this time on the subject of the reader's experience of fiction. Conrad's words stress the independence of the reader's temperament, and will, I hope, sharpen the student's senses for an intensive study of the novel.

Fiction . . . appeals to temperament. And . . . it must be . . . the appeal of one temperament to all the other innumerable temperaments whose . . . power endows passing events with their true meaning, and creates the moral, the emotional atmosphere of the place and time. Such an appeal to be effective must be an impression conveyed through the senses; and, in fact, it cannot be made in any other way, because temperament . . . is not amenable to persuasion. All art, therefore, appeals primarily to the senses, and the artistic aim when expressing itself in written words must also make its appeal through the senses, if its high desire is to reach the spring of responsive emotions.

(Joseph Conrad, Preface to
The Nigger of the 'Narcissus')

HEART OF DARKNESS

darkness of conquered countries
darkness in mind of man
light - deceptive glow of
                    civilization

imperialism is a cloak
    for plunder

HEART OF DARKNESS

I

THE *Nellie*, a cruising yawl, swung to her anchor without
a flutter of the sails, and was at rest. The flood had made,
the wind was nearly calm, and being bound down the
river, the only thing for it was to come to and wait for the
turn of the tide.

The sea-reach of the Thames stretched before us like
the beginning of an interminable waterway. In the offing
the sea and the sky were welded together without a joint,
and in the luminous space the tanned sails of the barges
drifting up with the tide seemed to stand still in red clusters
of canvas sharply peaked, with gleams of varnished sprits.
A haze rested on the low shores that ran out to sea in
vanishing flatness. The air was dark above Gravesend,
and farther back still seemed condensed into a mournful
gloom, brooding motionless over the biggest, and the
greatest, town on earth.

The Director of Companies was our captain and our
host. We four affectionately watched his back as he stood
in the bows looking to seaward. On the whole river there
was nothing that looked half so nautical. He resembled a
pilot, which to a seaman is trustworthiness personified. It
was difficult to realize his work was not out there in the
luminous estuary, but behind him, within the brooding
gloom.

Between us there was, as I have already said somewhere,
the bond of the sea. Besides holding our hearts together
through long periods of separation, it had the effect of

1st narrator

making us tolerant of each other's yarns—and even convictions. The Lawyer—the best of old fellows—had, because of his many years and many virtues, the only cushion on deck, and was lying on the only rug. The Accountant had brought out already a box of dominoes, and was toying architecturally with the bones. Marlow sat cross-legged right aft, leaning against the mizzen-mast. He had sunken cheeks, a yellow complexion, a straight back, an ascetic aspect, and, with his arms dropped, the palms of hands outwards, resembled an idol. The director, satisfied the anchor had good hold, made his way aft and sat down amongst us. We exchanged a few words lazily. Afterwards there was silence on board the yacht. For some reason or other we did not begin that game of dominoes. We felt meditative, and fit for nothing but placid staring. The day was ending in a serenity of still and exquisite brilliance. The water shone pacifically; the sky, without a speck, was a benign immensity of unstained light; the very mist on the Essex marshes was like a gauzy and radiant fabric, hung from the wooded rises inland, and draping the low shores in diaphanous folds. Only the gloom to the west, brooding over the upper reaches, became more sombre every minute, as if angered by the approach of the sun.

And at last, in its curved and imperceptible fall, the sun sank low, and from glowing white changed to a dull red without rays and without heat, as if about to go out suddenly, stricken to death by the touch of that gloom brooding over a crowd of men.

Forthwith a change came over the waters, and the serenity became less brilliant but more profound. The old river in its broad reach rested unruffled at the decline of day, after ages of good service done to the race that peopled its banks, spread out in the tranquil dignity of a waterway leading to the uttermost ends of the earth. We

looked at the venerable stream, not in the vivid flush of a
short day that comes and departs for ever, but in the august
light of abiding memories. And indeed nothing is easier
for a man who has, as the phrase goes, 'followed the sea'
with reverence and affection, than to evoke the great
spirit of the past upon the lower reaches of the Thames.
The tidal current runs to and fro in its unceasing service,
crowded with memories of men and ships it had borne to
the rest of home or to the battles of the sea. It had known
and served all the men of whom the nation is proud, from
Sir Francis Drake to Sir John Franklin, knights all, titled
and untitled—the great knights-errant of the sea. It had
borne all the ships whose names are like jewels flashing
in the night of time, from the *Golden Hind* returning with
her round flanks full of treasure, to be visited by the
Queen's Highness and thus pass out of the gigantic tale,
to the *Erebus* and *Terror*, bound on other conquests—and
that never returned. It had known the ships and the men.
They had sailed from Deptford, from Greenwich, from
Erith—the adventurers and the settlers; kings' ships and
the ships of men on 'Change; captains, admirals, the dark
'interlopers' of the Eastern trade, and the commissioned
'generals' of East India fleets. Hunters for gold or pursuers
of fame, they all had gone out on that stream, bearing the
sword, and often the torch, messengers of the might within
the land, bearers of a spark from the sacred fire. What
greatness had not floated on the ebb of that river into the
mystery of an unknown earth! . . . The dreams of men, the
seed of commonwealths, the germs of empires.

The sun set; the dusk fell on the stream, and lights
began to appear along the shore. The Chapman lighthouse,
a three-legged thing erect on a mud-flat, shone strongly.
Lights of ships moved in the fairway—a great stir of lights
going up and going down. And farther west on the upper
reaches the place of the monstrous town was still marked

ominously on the sky, a brooding gloom in sunshine, a lurid glare under the stars.

'And this also', said Marlow suddenly, 'has been one of the dark places of the earth.'

He was the only man of us who still 'followed the sea'. The worst that could be said of him was that he did not represent his class. He was a seaman, but he was a wanderer, too, while most seamen lead, if one may so express it, a sedentary life. Their minds are of the stay-at-home order, and their home is always with them—the ship; and so is their country—the sea. One ship is very much like another, and the sea is always the same. In the immutability of their surroundings the foreign shores, the foreign faces, the changing immensity of life, glide past, veiled not by a sense of mystery but by a slightly disdainful ignorance; for there is nothing mysterious to a seaman unless it be the sea itself, which is the mistress of his existence and as inscrutable as Destiny. For the rest, after his hours of work, a casual stroll or a casual spree on shore suffices to unfold for him the secret of a whole continent, and generally he finds the secret not worth knowing. The yarns of seamen have a direct simplicity, the whole meaning of which lies within the shell of a cracked nut. But Marlow was not typical (if his propensity to spin yarns be excepted), and to him the meaning of an episode was not inside like a kernel but outside, enveloping the tale which brought it out only as a glow brings out a haze, in the likeness of one of these misty haloes that sometimes are made visible by the spectral illumination of moonshine.

His remark did not seem at all surprising. It was just like Marlow. It was accepted in silence. No one took the trouble to grunt even; and presently he said, very slow:

'I was thinking of very old times, when the Romans first came here, nineteen hundred years ago—the other day. . . . Light came out of this river since—you say

Knights? Yes; but it is like a running blaze on a plain, like a flash of lightning in the clouds. We live in the flicker —may it last as long as the old earth keeps rolling! But darkness was here yesterday. Imagine the feelings of a commander of a fine—what d'ye call 'em?—trireme in the Mediterranean, ordered suddenly to the north; run overland across the Gauls in a hurry; put in charge of one of these craft the legionaries—a wonderful lot of handy men they must have been, too—used to build, apparently by the hundred, in a month or two, if we may believe what we read. Imagine him here—the very end of the world, a sea the colour of lead, a sky the colour of smoke, a kind of ship about as rigid as a concertina—and going up this river with stores, or orders, or what you like. Sand-banks, marshes, forests, savages—precious little to eat fit for a civilized man, nothing but Thames water to drink. No Falernian wine here, no going ashore. Here and there a military camp lost in a wilderness, like a needle in a bundle of hay—cold, fog, tempests, disease, exile, and death—death skulking in the air, in the water, in the bush. They must have been dying like flies here. Oh yes —he did it. Did it very well, too, no doubt, and without thinking much about it either, except afterwards to brag of what he had gone through in his time, perhaps. They were men enough to face the darkness. And perhaps he was cheered by keeping his eye on a chance of promotion to the fleet at Ravenna by and by, if he had good friends in Rome and survived the awful climate. Or think of a decent young citizen in a toga—perhaps too much dice, you know—coming out here in the train of some prefect, or tax-gatherer, or trader even, to mend his fortunes. Land in a swamp, march through the woods, and in some inland post feel the savagery, the utter savagery, had closed round him—all that mysterious life of the wilderness that stirs in the forest, in the jungles, in the hearts of wild men.

There's no initiation either into such mysteries. He has to live in the midst of the incomprehensible, which is also detestable. And it has a fascination, too, that goes to work upon him. The fascination of the abomination—you know, imagine the growing regrets, the longing to escape, the powerless disgust, the surrender, the hate.'

He paused.

'Mind,' he began again, lifting one arm from the elbow, the palm of the hand outwards, so that, with his legs folded before him, he had the pose of a Buddha preaching in European clothes and without a lotus-flower, 'mind, none of us would feel exactly like this. What saves us is efficiency—the devotion to efficiency. But these chaps were not much account, really. They were no colonists; their administration was merely a squeeze, and nothing more, I suspect. They were conquerors, and for that you want only brute force—nothing to boast of, when you have it, since your strength is just an accident arising from the weakness of others. They grabbed what they could get for the sake of what was to be got. It was just robbery with violence, aggravated murder on a great scale, and men going at it blind—as is very proper for those who tackle a darkness. The conquest of the earth, which mostly means the taking it away from those who have a different complexion or slightly flatter noses than ourselves, is not a pretty thing when you look into it too much. What redeems it is the idea only. An idea at the back of it; not a sentimental pretence but an idea; and an unselfish belief in the idea—something you can set up, and bow down before, and offer a sacrifice to——'

He broke off. Flames glided in the river, small green flames, red flames, white flames, pursuing, overtaking, joining, crossing each other—then separating slowly or hastily. The traffic of the great city went on in the deepening night upon the sleepless river. We looked on, waiting patiently—there was nothing else to do till the end of the flood; but it was only after a long silence, when he said, in a hesitating voice, 'I suppose you fellows remember I did once turn fresh-water sailor for a bit', that we knew we were fated, before the ebb began to run, to hear about one of Marlow's inconclusive experiences.

'I don't want to bother you much with what happened to me personally,' he began, showing in this remark the weakness of many tellers of tales who seem so often unaware of what their audience would best like to hear; 'yet to understand the effect of it on me you ought to know how I got out there, what I saw, how I went up that river to the place where I first met the poor chap. It was the farthest point of navigation and the culminating point of my experience. It seemed somehow to throw a kind of light on everything about me—and into my thoughts. It was sombre enough, too—and pitiful—not extraordinary in any way—not very clear either. No, not very clear. And yet it seemed to throw a kind of light.

'I had then, as you remember, just returned to London after a lot of Indian Ocean, Pacific, China Seas—a regular dose of the East—six years or so, and I was loafing about, hindering you fellows in your work and invading your homes, just as though I had got a heavenly mission to civilize you. It was very fine for a time, but after a bit I did get tired of resting. Then I began to look for a ship— I should think the hardest work on earth. But the ships wouldn't even look at me. And I got tired of that game, too.

'Now when I was a little chap I had a passion for maps. I would look for hours at South America, or Africa, or Australia, and lose myself in all the glories of exploration. At that time there were many blank spaces on the earth, and when I saw one that looked particularly inviting on a map (but they all look that) I would put my finger on it and say, When I grow up I will go there. The North Pole was one of these places, I remember. Well, I haven't been there yet, and shall not try now. The glamour's off. Other places were scattered about the equator, and in every sort of latitude all over the two hemispheres. I have been in some of them, and . . . well, we won't talk about that. But there was one yet—the biggest, the most blank, so to speak—that I had a hankering after.

'True, by this time it was not a blank space any more. It had got filled since my boyhood with rivers and lakes and names. It had ceased to be a blank space of delightful mystery—a white patch for a boy to dream gloriously over. It had become a place of darkness. But there was in it one river especially, a mighty big river, that you could see on the map, resembling an immense snake uncoiled, with its head in the sea, its body at rest curving afar over a vast country, and its tail lost in the depths of the land. And as I looked at the map of it in a shop window, it fascinated me as a snake would a bird—a silly little bird. Then I remembered there was a big concern, a Company for trade on that river. Dash it all! I thought to myself, they can't trade without using some kind of craft on that lot of fresh water—steamboats! Why shouldn't I try to get charge of one? I went on along Fleet Street, but could not shake off the idea. The snake had charmed me.

'You understand it was a continental concern, that trading society; but I have a lot of relations living on the Continent, because it's cheap and not so nasty as it looks, they say.

'I am sorry to own I began to worry them. This was already a fresh departure for me. I was not used to get things that way, you know. I always went my own road and on my own legs where I had a mind to go. I wouldn't have believed it of myself; but, then—you see—I felt somehow I must get there by hook or by crook. So I worried them. The men said, "My dear fellow", and did nothing. Then—would you believe it?—I tried the women. I, Charlie Marlow, set the women to work—to get a job. Heavens! Well, you see, the notion drove me. I had an aunt, a dear enthusiastic soul. She wrote: "It will be delightful. I am ready to do anything, anything for you. It is a glorious idea. I know the wife of a very high personage in the Administration, and also a man who has lots of influence with", etc. etc. She was determined to make no end of fuss to get me appointed skipper of a river steamboat, if such was my fancy.

'I got my appointment—of course; and I got it very quick. It appears the Company had received news that one of their captains had been killed in a scuffle with the natives. This was my chance, and it made me the more anxious to go. It was only months and months afterwards, when I made the attempt to recover what was left of the body, that I heard the original quarrel arose from a misunderstanding about some hens. Yes, two black hens. Fresleven—that was the fellow's name, a Dane—thought himself wronged somehow in the bargain, so he went ashore and started to hammer the chief of the village with a stick. Oh, it didn't surprise me in the least to hear this, and at the same time to be told that Fresleven was the gentlest, quietest creature that ever walked on two legs. No doubt he was; but he had been a couple of years already out there engaged in the noble cause, you know, and he probably felt the need at last of asserting his self-respect in some way. Therefore he whacked the old negro mercilessly, while a big crowd of his people watched him, thunderstruck, till some man—I was told the chief's son—in desperation at hearing the old chap yell, made a tentative jab with a spear at the white man—and of course it went quite easy between the shoulder-blades. Then the whole population cleared into the forest,

*B

expecting all kinds of calamities to happen, while, on the other hand, the steamer Fresleven commanded left also in a bad panic, in charge of the engineer, I believe. Afterwards nobody seemed to trouble much about Fresleven's remains, till I got out and stepped into his shoes. I couldn't let it rest, though; but when an opportunity offered at last to meet my predecessor, the grass growing through his ribs was tall enough to hide his bones. They were all there. The supernatural being had not been touched after he fell. And the village was deserted, the huts gaped black, rotting, all askew within the fallen enclosures. A calamity had come to it, sure enough. The people had vanished. Mad terror had scattered them, men, women, and children, through the bush, and they had never returned. What became of the hens I don't know either. I should think the cause of progress got them, anyhow. However, through this glorious affair I got my appointment, before I had fairly begun to hope for it.

'I flew around like mad to get ready, and before forty-eight hours I was crossing the Channel to show myself to my employers, and sign the contract. In a very few hours I arrived in a city that always makes me think of a whited sepulchre. Prejudice no doubt. I had no difficulty in finding the Company's offices. It was the biggest thing in the town, and everybody I met was full of it. They were going to run an over-sea empire, and make no end of coin by trade.

'A narrow and deserted street in deep shadow, high houses, innumerable windows with venetian blinds, a dead silence, grass sprouting between the stones, imposing carriage archways right and left, immense double doors standing ponderously ajar. I slipped through one of these cracks, went up a swept and ungarnished staircase, as arid as a desert, and opened the first door I came to. Two women, one fat and the other slim, sat on straw-bottomed chairs, knitting black wool. The slim one got up and walked straight at me—still knitting with down-cast eyes —and only just as I began to think of getting out of her way, as you would for a somnambulist, stood still, and looked up. Her dress was as plain as an umbrella-cover, and she turned round without a word and preceded me into a waiting-room. I gave my name, and looked about. Deal table in the middle, plain chairs all round the walls, on one end a large shining map, marked with all the colours of a rainbow. There was a vast amount of red— good to see at any time, because one knows that some real work is done in there, a deuce of a lot of blue, a little green, smears of orange, and, on the East Coast, a purple patch, to show where the jolly pioneers of progress drink the jolly lager-beer. However, I wasn't going into any of these. I was going into the yellow. Dead in the centre. And the river was there—fascinating—deadly—like a snake. Ough! A door opened, a white-haired secretarial head, but wearing a compassionate expression, appeared, and a skinny forefinger beckoned me into the sanctuary. Its light was dim, and a heavy writing-desk squatted in the middle. From behind that structure came out an impression of pale plumpness in a frock-coat. The great man himself. He was five feet six, I should judge, and had his grip on the handle-end of ever so many millions. He shook hands, I fancy, murmured vaguely, was satisfied with my French. *Bon voyage.*

'In about forty-five seconds I found myself again in the waiting-room with the compassionate secretary, who, full of desolation and sympathy, made me sign some document. I believe I undertook amongst other things not to disclose any trade secrets. Well, I am not going to.

'I began to feel slightly uneasy. You know I am not used to such ceremonies, and there was something ominous in the atmosphere. It was just as though I had been let into some conspiracy—I don't know—something not quite right; and I was glad to get out. In the outer room the two women knitted black wool feverishly. People were arriving, and the younger one was walking back and forth introducing them. The old one sat on her chair. Her flat cloth slippers were propped up on a foot-warmer, and a cat reposed on her lap. She wore a starched white affair on her head, had a wart on one cheek, and silver-rimmed spectacles hung on the tip of her nose. She glanced at me above the glasses. The swift and indifferent placidity of that look troubled me. Two youths with foolish and cheery countenances were being piloted over, and she threw at them the same quick glance of unconcerned wisdom. She seemed to know all about them and about me, too. An eerie feeling came over me. She seemed uncanny and fateful. Often far away there I thought of these two, guarding the door of Darkness, knitting black wool as for a warm pall, one introducing, introducing continuously to the unknown, the other scrutinizing the cheery and foolish faces with unconcerned old eyes. *Ave!* Old knitter of black wool. *Morituri te salutant.* Not many of those she looked at ever saw her again—not half, by a long way.

'There was yet a visit to the doctor. "A simple formality," assured me the secretary, with an air of taking an immense part in all my sorrows. Accordingly a young chap wearing his hat over the left eyebrow, some clerk I suppose—there must have been clerks in the business, though the house was as still as a house in a city of the dead—came from somewhere upstairs, and led me forth. He was shabby and careless, with ink stains on the sleeves of his jacket, and his cravat was large and billowy, under a chin shaped like the toe of an old boot. It was a little too early for the doctor, so I proposed a drink, and thereupon he developed a vein of joviality. As we sat over our vermouths he glorified the Company's business, and by and by I expressed casually my surprise at him not going out there. He became very cool and collected all at once. "I am not such a fool as I look, quoth Plato to his disciples," he said sententiously, emptied his glass with great resolution, and we rose.

'The old doctor felt my pulse, evidently thinking of something else the while. "Good, good for there," he mumbled, and then with a certain eagerness asked me whether I would let him measure my head. Rather surprised, I said Yes, when he produced a thing like calipers and got the dimensions back and front and every way, taking notes carefully. He was an unshaven little man in a threadbare coat like a gaberdine, with his feet in slippers, and I thought him a harmless fool. "I always ask leave, in the interests of science, to measure the crania of those going out there," he said. "And when they come back, too?" I asked. "Oh, I never see them," he remarked; "and, moreover, the changes take place inside, you know." He smiled, as if at some quiet joke. "So you are going out there. Famous. Interesting, too." He gave me a searching glance, and made another note. "Ever any madness in your family?" he asked, in a matter-of-fact tone. I felt very annoyed. "Is that question in the interests of science, too?" "It would be", he said, without taking notice of my irritation, "interesting for science to watch the mental changes of individuals, on the spot, but——" "Are you an alienist?" I interrupted. "Every doctor should be—a little," answered that original, imperturbably. "I have a little theory which you Messieurs who go out there must help me to prove. This is my share in the advantages my country shall reap from the possession of such a magnificent dependency. The mere wealth I leave to others. Pardon my questions, but you are the first Englishman coming under my observation . . ." I hastened to assure him I was not in the least typical. "If I were", said I, "I wouldn't be talking like this with you." "What you say is rather profound, and probably erroneous," he said, with a laugh. "Avoid irritation more than exposure to the sun. *Adieu.* How do you English say, eh? Goodbye. Ah! Goodbye. *Adieu.* In the tropics one must before everything keep calm." He lifted a warning forefinger. . . . "*Du calme, du calme. Adieu.*"

'One thing more remained to do—say goodbye to my excellent aunt. I found her triumphant. I had a cup of tea—the last decent cup of tea for many days—and in a room that most soothingly looked just as you would expect a lady's drawing-room to look, we had a long quiet chat by the fireside. In the course of these confidences it became quite plain to me I had been represented to the wife of the high dignitary, and goodness knows to how many more people besides, as an exceptional and gifted creature—a piece of good fortune for the Company—a man you don't get hold of every day. Good heavens! and I was going to take charge of a twopenny-halfpenny river steamboat with a penny whistle attached! It appeared, however, I was also one of the Workers, with a capital—you know. Something like an emissary of light, something like a lower sort of apostle. There had been a lot of such rot let loose in print and talk just about that time, and the excellent woman, living right in the rush of all that humbug, got carried off her feet. She talked about "weaning those ignorant millions from their horrid ways", till, upon my word, she made me quite uncomfortable. I ventured to hint that the Company was run for profit.

'"You forget, dear Charlie, that the labourer is worthy of his hire," she said, brightly. It's queer how out of touch with truth women are. They live in a world of their own, and there has never been anything like it, and never can be. It is too beautiful altogether, and if they were to set it up it would go to pieces before the first sunset. Some confounded fact we men have been living contentedly with ever since the day of creation would start up and knock the whole thing over.

'After this I got embraced, told to wear flannel, be sure to write often, and so on—and I left. In the street—I don't know why—a queer feeling came to me that I was an impostor. Odd thing that I, who used to clear out for any part of the world at twenty-four hours' notice, with less thought than most men give to the crossing of a street, had a moment—I won't say of hesitation, but of startled pause, before this commonplace affair. The best way I can explain it to you is by saying that, for a second or two, I felt as though, instead of going to the centre of a continent, I were about to set off for the centre of the earth.

'I left in a French steamer, and she called in at every blamed port they have out there, for, as far as I could see, the sole purpose of landing soldiers and custom-house officers. I watched the coast. Watching a coast as it slips by the ship is like thinking about an enigma. There it is before you—smiling, frowning, inviting, grand, mean, insipid, or savage, and always mute with an air of whispering, Come and find out. This one was almost featureless, as if still in the making, with an aspect of monotonous grimness. The edge of a colossal jungle, so dark-green as to be almost black, fringed with white surf, ran straight, like a ruled line, far, far away along a blue sea whose glitter was blurred by a creeping mist. The sun was fierce, the land seemed to glisten and drip with steam. Here and there greyish-whitish specks showed up clustered inside the white surf, with a flag flying above them perhaps. Settlements some centuries old, and still no bigger than pin-heads on the untouched expanse of their background. We pounded along, stopped, landed soldiers; went on, landed custom-house clerks to levy toll in what looked like a God-forsaken wilderness, with a tin shed and a flag-pole lost in it; landed more soldiers—to take care of the custom-house clerks, presumably. Some, I heard, got drowned in the surf; but whether they did or not, nobody seemed particularly to care. They were just flung out there, and on we went. Every day the coast looked the same, as though we had not moved; but we passed various places—trading places—with names like Gran' Bassam, Little Popo; names that seemed to belong to some sordid farce acted in front of a sinister back-cloth. The idleness of a passenger, my isolation amongst all these men with whom I had no point of contact, the oily and languid sea, the uniform sombreness of the coast, seemed to keep me away from the truth of things, within the toil of a mournful and senseless delusion. The voice of the surf heard now and then was a positive pleasure, like the speech of a brother. It was something natural, that had its reason, that had a meaning. Now and then a boat from the shore gave one a momentary contact with reality. It was paddled by black fellows. You could see from afar the white of their eyeballs glistening. They shouted, sang; their bodies streamed with perspiration; they had faces like grotesque masks—these chaps; but they had bone, muscle, a wild vitality, an intense energy of movement, that was as natural and true as the surf along their coast. They wanted no excuse for being there. They were a great comfort to look at. For a time I would feel I belonged still to a world of straight-forward facts; but the feeling would not last long. Something would turn up to scare it away. Once, I remember, we came upon a man-of-war anchored off the coast. There wasn't even a shed there, and she was shelling the bush. It appears the French had one of their wars going on there-abouts. Her ensign dropped limp like a rag; the muzzles of the long six-inch guns stuck out all over the low hull; the greasy, slimy swell swung her up lazily and let her down, swaying her thin masts. In the empty immensity

of earth, sky, and water, there she was, incomprehensible,
firing into a continent. Pop, would go one of the six-inch
guns; a small flame would dart and vanish, a little white
smoke would disappear, a tiny projectile would give a
feeble screech—and nothing happened. Nothing could
happen. There was a touch of insanity in the proceeding,
a sense of lugubrious drollery in the sight; and it was not
dissipated by somebody on board assuring me earnestly
there was a camp of natives—he called them enemies!—
hidden out of sight somewhere.

'We gave her her letters (I heard the men in that lonely
ship were dying of fever at the rate of three a day) and
went on. We called at some more places with farcical
names, where the merry dance of death and trade goes
on in a still and earthy atmosphere as of an overheated
catacomb; all along the formless coast bordered by dangerous surf, as if Nature herself had tried to ward off intruders;
in and out of rivers, streams of death in life, whose banks
were rotting into mud, whose waters, thickened into slime,
invaded the contorted mangroves, that seemed to writhe
at us in the extremity of an impotent despair. Nowhere
did we stop long enough to get a particularized impression,
but the general sense of vague and oppressive wonder
grew upon me. It was like a weary pilgrimage amongst
hints for nightmares.

'It was upward of thirty days before I saw the mouth
of the big river. We anchored off the seat of the government. But my work would not begin till some two hundred
miles farther on. So as soon as I could I made a start for a
place thirty miles higher up.

'I had my passage on a little sea-going steamer. Her
captain was a Swede, and knowing me for a seaman,
invited me on the bridge. He was a young man, lean, fair,
and morose, with lanky hair and a shuffling gait. As
we left the miserable little wharf, he tossed his head

contemptuously at the shore. "Been living there?" he asked. I said, "Yes." "Fine lot these government chaps —are they not?" he went on, speaking English with great precision and considerable bitterness. "It is funny what some people will do for a few francs a month. I wonder what becomes of that kind when it goes up-country?" I said to him I expected to see that soon. "So-o-o!" he exclaimed. He shuffled athwart, keeping one eye ahead vigilantly. "Don't be too sure," he continued. "The other day I took up a man who hanged himself on the road. He was a Swede, too." "Hanged himself! Why, in God's name?" I cried. He kept on looking out watchfully. "Who knows? The sun too much for him, or the country perhaps."

'At last we opened a reach. A rocky cliff appeared, mounds of turned-up earth by the shore, houses on a hill, others with iron roofs, amongst a waste of excavations, or hanging to the declivity. A continuous noise of the rapids above hovered over this scene of inhabited devastation. A lot of people, mostly black and naked, moved about like ants. A jetty projected into the river. A blinding sunlight drowned all this at times in a sudden recrudescence of glare. "There's your Company's station," said the Swede, pointing to three wooden barrack-like structures on the rocky slope. "I will send your things up. Four boxes did you say? So. Farewell."

'I came upon a boiler wallowing in the grass, then found a path leading up the hill. It turned aside for the boulders, and also for an undersized railway truck lying there on its back with its wheels in the air. One was off. The thing looked as dead as the carcass of some animal. I came upon more pieces of decaying machinery, a stack of rusty rails. To the left a clump of trees made a shady spot, where dark things seemed to stir feebly. I blinked, the path was steep. A horn tooted to the right, and I saw the black

people run. A heavy and dull detonation shook the ground,
a puff of smoke came out of the cliff, and that was all. No
change appeared on the face of the rock. They were
building a railway. The cliff was not in the way or
anything; but this objectless blasting was all the work
going on.

'A slight clinking behind me made me turn my head.
Six black men advanced in a file, toiling up the path.
They walked erect and slow, balancing small baskets full
of earth on their heads, and the clink kept time with their
footsteps. Black rags were wound round their loins, and
the short ends behind waggled to and fro like tails. I could
see every rib, the joints of their limbs were like knots in a
rope; each had an iron collar on his neck, and all were
connected together with a chain whose bights swung
between them, rhythmically clinking. Another report
from the cliff made me think suddenly of that ship of war
I had seen firing into a continent. It was the same kind of
ominous voice; but these men could by no stretch of
imagination be called enemies. They were called criminals,
and the outraged law, like the bursting shells, had come
to them, an insoluble mystery from the sea. All their meagre
breasts panted together, the violently dilated nostrils
quivered, the eyes stared stonily uphill. They passed me
within six inches, without a glance, with that complete,
deathlike indifference of unhappy savages. Behind this
raw matter one of the reclaimed, the product of the new
forces at work, strolled despondently, carrying a rifle by
its middle. He had a uniform jacket with one button off,
and seeing a white man on the path, hoisted his weapon
to his shoulder with alacrity. This was simple prudence,
white men being so much alike at a distance that he could
not tell who I might be. He was speedily reassured, and
with a large, white, rascally grin, and a glance at his
charge, seemed to take me into partnership in his exalted

trust. After all, I also was a part of the great cause of these high and just proceedings.

'Instead of going up, I turned and descended to the left. My idea was to let that chain-gang get out of sight before I climbed the hill. You know I am not particularly tender; I've had to strike and to fend off. I've had to resist and to attack sometimes—that's only one way of resisting—without counting the exact cost, according to the demands of such sort of life as I had blundered into. I've seen the devil of violence, and the devil of greed, and the devil of hot desire; but, by all the stars! these were strong, lusty, red-eyed devils, that swayed and drove men —men, I tell you. But as I stood on this hillside, I foresaw that in the blinding sunshine of that land I would become acquainted with a flabby, pretending, weak-eyed devil of a rapacious and pitiless folly. How insidious he could be, too, I was only to find out several months later and a thousand miles farther. For a moment I stood appalled, as though by a warning. Finally I descended the hill, obliquely, towards the trees I had seen.

'I avoided a vast artificial hole somebody had been digging on the slope, the purpose of which I found it impossible to divine. It wasn't a quarry or a sandpit, anyhow. It was just a hole. It might have been connected with the philanthropic desire of giving the criminals something to do. I don't know. Then I nearly fell into a very narrow ravine, almost no more than a scar in the hillside. I discovered that a lot of imported drainage pipes for the settlement had been tumbled in there. There wasn't one that was not broken. It was a wanton smash-up. At last I got under the trees. My purpose was to stroll into the shade for a moment; but no sooner within than it seemed to me I had stepped into the gloomy circle of some Inferno. The rapids were near, and an uninterrupted, uniform, headlong, rushing noise filled the mournful stillness of the grove, where not a breath stirred, not a leaf moved, with a mysterious sound—as though the tearing pace of the launched earth had suddenly become audible.

'Black shapes crouched, lay, sat between the trees leaning against the trunks, clinging to the earth, half coming out, half effaced within the dim light, in all the attitudes of pain, abandonment, and despair. Another mine on the cliff went off, followed by a slight shudder of the soil under my feet. The work was going on. The work! And this was the place where some of the helpers had withdrawn to die.

'They were dying slowly—it was very clear. They were not enemies, they were not criminals, they were nothing earthly now—nothing but black shadows of disease and starvation, lying confusedly in the greenish gloom. Brought from all the recesses of the coast in all the legality of time contracts, lost in uncongenial surroundings, fed on unfamiliar food, they sickened, became inefficient, and were then allowed to crawl away and rest. These moribund shapes were free as air—and nearly as thin. I began to distinguish the gleam of the eyes under the trees. Then, glancing down, I saw a face near my hand. The black bones reclined at full length with one shoulder against the tree, and slowly the eyelids rose and the sunken eyes looked up at me, enormous and vacant, a kind of blind, white flicker in the depths of the orbs, which died out slowly. The man seemed young—almost a boy—but you know with them it's hard to tell. I found nothing else to do but to offer him one of my good Swede's ship's biscuits I had in my pocket. The fingers closed slowly on it and held—there was no other movement and no other glance. He had tied a bit of white worsted round his neck. Why? Where did he get it? Was it a badge—an ornament—a charm—a propitiatory act? Was there any idea at all connected with it? It looked startling round his black neck, this bit of white thread from beyond the seas.

'Near the same tree two more bundles of acute angles sat with their legs drawn up. One, with his chin propped on his knees, stared at nothing, in an intolerable and appalling manner: his brother phantom rested its forehead, as if overcome with a great weariness; and all about others were scattered in every pose of contorted collapse, as in some picture of a massacre or a pestilence. While I stood horror-struck, one of these creatures rose to his hands and knees, and went off on all fours towards the river to drink. He lapped out of his hand, then sat up in the sunlight, crossing his shins in front of him, and after a time let his woolly head fall on his breastbone.

'I didn't want any more loitering in the shade, and I made haste towards the station. When near the buildings I met a white man, in such an unexpected elegance of get-up that in the first moment I took him for a sort of vision. I saw a high starched collar, white cuffs, a light alpaca jacket, snowy trousers, a clear necktie, and varnished boots. No hat. Hair parted, brushed, oiled, under a green-lined parasol held in a big white hand. He was amazing, and had a penholder behind his ear.

'I shook hands with this miracle, and I learned he was the Company's chief accountant, and that all the book-keeping was done at this station. He had come out for a moment, he said, "to get a breath of fresh air". The expression sounded wonderfully odd, with its suggestion of sedentary desk life. I wouldn't have mentioned the fellow to you at all, only it was from his lips that I first heard the name of the man who is so indissolubly connected with the memories of that time. Moreover, I respected the fellow. Yes; I respected his collars, his vast cuffs, his brushed hair. His appearance was certainly that of a hairdresser's dummy; but in the great demoralization of the land he kept up his appearance. That's backbone. His starched collars and got-up shirt-fronts were achievements of character. He had been out nearly three years; and, later, I could not help asking him how he managed to sport such linen. He had just the faintest blush, and said modestly: "I've been teaching one of the native women about the station. It was difficult. She had a distaste for the work." Thus this man had verily accomplished something. And he was devoted to his books, which were in apple-pie order.

'Everything else in the station was in a muddle—heads, things, buildings. Strings of dusty negroes with splay feet arrived and departed; a stream of manufactured goods, rubbishy cottons, beads, and brass wire set into the depths of darkness, and in return came a precious trickle of ivory.

'I had to wait in the station for ten days—an eternity. I lived in a hut in the yard, but to be out of the chaos I would sometimes get into the accountant's office. It was built of horizontal planks, and so badly put together that, as he bent over his high desk, he was barred from neck to heels with narrow strips of sunlight. There was no need to open the big shutter to see. It was hot there, too; big flies buzzed fiendishly, and did not sting, but stabbed. I sat generally on the floor, while, of faultless appearance (and even slightly scented), perching on a high stool, he wrote, he wrote. Sometimes he stood up for exercise. When a truckle-bed with a sick man (some invalid agent from up-country) was put in there, he exhibited a gentle annoyance. "The groans of this sick person", he said, "distract my attention. And without that it is extremely difficult to guard against clerical errors in this climate."

'One day he remarked, without lifting his head: "In the interior you will no doubt meet Mr Kurtz." On my asking who Mr Kurtz was, he said he was a first-class agent; and seeing my disappointment at this information, he added slowly, laying down his pen: "He is a very remarkable person." Further questions elicited from him that Mr Kurtz was at present in charge of a trading-post, a very important one, in the true ivory country, at "the very bottom of there. Sends in as much ivory as all the others put together. . . ." He began to write again. The sick man was too ill to groan. The flies buzzed in a great peace.

'Suddenly there was a growing murmur of voices and a great tramping of feet. A caravan had come in. A violent babble of uncouth sounds burst out on the other side of the planks. All the carriers were speaking together, and in the midst of the uproar the lamentable voice of the chief agent was heard "giving it up" tearfully for the twentieth time that day. . . . He rose slowly. "What a frightful row," he said. He crossed the room gently to look at the sick man, and, returning, said to me: "He does not hear." "What! Dead?" I asked, startled. "No, not yet," he answered, with great composure. Then, alluding with a toss of the head to the tumult in the station yard: "When one has got to make correct entries, one comes to hate those savages—hate them to the death." He remained thoughtful for a moment. "When you see Mr Kurtz," he went on, "tell him from me that everything here"—he glanced at the desk—"is very satisfactory. I don't like to write to him—with those messengers of ours you never know who may get hold of your letter—at that Central Station." He stared at me for a moment with his mild, bulging eyes. "Oh, he will go far, very far," he began again. "He will be a somebody in the Administration before long. They, above—the Council in Europe, you know—mean him to be."

'He turned to his work. The noise outside had ceased, and presently in going out I stopped at the door. In the steady buzz of flies the homeward-bound agent was lying flushed and insensible; the other, bent over his books, was making correct entries of perfectly correct transactions; and fifty feet below the doorstep I could see the still tree tops of the grove of death.

'Next day I left that station at last, with a caravan of sixty men, for a two-hundred-mile tramp.

'No use telling you much about that. Paths, paths, everywhere; a stamped-in network of paths spreading over the empty land, through long grass, through burnt grass, through thickets, down and up chilly ravines, up and down stony hills ablaze with heat; and a solitude, a solitude, nobody, not a hut. The population had cleared out a long time ago. Well, if a lot of mysterious negroes armed with all kinds of fearful weapons suddenly took to travelling on the road between Deal and Gravesend, catching the yokels right and left to carry heavy loads for them, I fancy every farm and cottage thereabouts would get empty very soon. Only here the dwellings were gone, too. Still I passed through several abandoned villages. There's something pathetically childish in the ruins of grass walls. Day after day, with the stamp and shuffle of sixty pair of bare feet behind me, each pair under a 60-lb. load. Camp, cook, sleep, strike camp, march. Now and then a carrier dead in harness, at rest in the long grass near the path, with an empty water-gourd and his long staff lying by his side. A great silence around and above. Perhaps on some quiet night the tremor of far-off drums, sinking, swelling, a tremor vast, faint; a sound weird, appealing, suggestive, and wild—and perhaps with as profound a meaning as the sound of bells in a Christian country. Once a white man in an unbuttoned uniform, camping on the path with an armed escort of lank Zanzibaris, very hospitable and festive—not to say drunk. Was looking after the upkeep of the road, he declared.

Can't say I saw any road or any upkeep, unless the body
of a middle-aged negro, with a bullet hole in the forehead,
upon which I absolutely stumbled three miles farther on,
may be considered as a permanent improvement. I had a
white companion, too, not a bad chap, but rather too fleshy
and with the exasperating habit of fainting on the hot
hillsides, miles away from the least bit of shade and water.
Annoying, you know, to hold your own coat like a parasol
over a man's head while he is coming to. I couldn't help
asking him once what he meant by coming there at all.
"To make money, of course. What do you think?" he
said, scornfully. Then he got fever, and had to be carried
in a hammock slung under a pole. As he weighed sixteen
stone I had no end of rows with the carriers. They jibbed,
ran away, sneaked off with their loads in the night—quite
a mutiny. So, one evening, I made a speech in English
with gestures, not one of which was lost to the sixty pairs
of eyes before me, and the next morning I started the
hammock off in front all right. An hour afterwards I came
upon the whole concern wrecked in a bush—man, hammock, groans, blankets, horrors. The heavy pole had
skinned his poor nose. He was very anxious for me to kill
somebody, but there wasn't the shadow of a carrier near.
I remember the old doctor: " It would be interesting for
science to watch the mental changes of individuals, on
the spot." I felt I was becoming scientifically interesting.
However, all that is to no purpose. On the fifteenth day I
came in sight of the big river again, and hobbled into the
Central Station. It was on a backwater surrounded by
scrub and forest, with a pretty border of smelly mud on
one side, and on the three others enclosed by a crazy fence
of rushes. A neglected gap was all the gate it had, and the
first glance at the place was enough to let you see the
flabby devil was running that show. White men with long
staves in their hands appeared languidly from amongst

the buildings, strolling up to take a look at me, and then retired out of sight somewhere. One of them, a stout, excitable chap with black moustaches, informed me with great volubility and many digressions, as soon as I told him who I was, that my steamer was at the bottom of the river. I was thunderstruck. What, how, why? Oh, it was "all right". The "manager himself" was there. All quite correct. "Everybody had behaved splendidly! splendidly!"—"You must", he said in agitation, "go and see the general manager at once. He is waiting!"

'I did not see the real significance of that wreck at once. I fancy I see it now, but I am not sure—not at all. Certainly the affair was too stupid—when I think of it—to be altogether natural. Still . . . but at the moment it presented itself simply as a confounded nuisance. The steamer was sunk. They had started two days before in a sudden hurry up the river with the manager on board, in charge of some volunteer skipper, and before they had been out three hours they tore the bottom out of her on stones, and she sank near the south bank. I asked myself what I was to do there, now my boat was lost. As a matter of fact, I had plenty to do in fishing my command out of the river. I had to set about it the very next day. That, and the repairs when I brought the pieces to the station, took some months.

'My first interview with the manager was curious. He did not ask me to sit down after my twenty-mile walk that morning. He was commonplace in complexion, in feature, in manners, and in voice. He was of middle size and of ordinary build. His eyes, of the usual blue, were perhaps remarkably cold, and he certainly could make his glance fall on one as trenchant and heavy as an axe. But even at these times the rest of his person seemed to disclaim the intention. Otherwise there was only an indefinable, faint expression of his lips, something stealthy—a smile—not a

smile—I remember it, but I can't explain. It was unconscious, this smile was, though just after he had said
something it got intensified for an instant. It came at the
end of his speeches like a seal applied on the words to make
the meaning of the commonest phrase appear absolutely
inscrutable. He was a common trader, from his youth up
employed in these parts—nothing more. He was obeyed,
yet he inspired neither love nor fear, nor even respect. He
inspired uneasiness. That was it! Uneasiness. Not a
definite mistrust—just uneasiness—nothing more. You
have no idea how effective such a . . . a . . . faculty can be.
He had no genius for organizing, for initiative, or for order
even. That was evident in such things as the deplorable
state of the station. He had no learning, and no intelligence. His position had come to him—why? Perhaps
because he was never ill. . . . He had served three terms
of three years out there. . . . Because triumphant health in
the general rout of constitutions is a kind of power in itself.
When he went home on leave he rioted on a large scale—
pompously. Jack ashore—with a difference—in externals
only. This one could gather from his casual talk. He
originated nothing, he could keep the routine going—
that's all. But he was great. He was great by this little
thing that it was impossible to tell what could control
such a man. He never gave that secret away. Perhaps there
was nothing within him. Such a suspicion made one pause
—for out there there were no external checks. Once when
various tropical diseases had laid low almost every "agent"
in the station, he was heard to say: "Men who come out
here should have no entrails." He sealed the utterance
with that smile of his, as though it had been a door opening
into a darkness he had in his keeping. You fancied you had
seen things—but the seal was on. When annoyed at meal
times by the constant quarrels of the white men about
precedence, he ordered an immense round table to be

made, for which a special house had to be built. This was the station's mess-room. Where he sat was the first place—the rest were nowhere. One felt this to be his unalterable conviction. He was neither civil nor uncivil. He was quiet. He allowed his "boy"—an overfed young negro from the coast—to treat the white men, under his very eyes, with provoking insolence.

'He began to speak as soon as he saw me. I had been very long on the road. He could not wait. Had to start without me. The upriver stations had to be relieved. There had been so many delays already that he did not know who was dead and who was alive, and how they got on—and so on, and so on. He paid no attention to my explanations, and, playing with a stick of sealing-wax, repeated several times that the situation was "very grave, very grave". There were rumours that a very important station was in jeopardy, and its chief, Mr Kurtz, was ill. Hoped it was not true. Mr Kurtz was . . . I felt weary and irritable. Hang Kurtz, I thought. I interrupted him by saying I had heard of Mr Kurtz on the coast. "Ah! So they talk of him down there," he murmured to himself. Then he began again, assuring me Mr Kurtz was the best agent he had, an exceptional man, of the greatest importance to the Company; therefore I could understand his anxiety. He was, he said, "very, very uneasy". Certainly he fidgeted on his chair a good deal, exclaimed, "Ah, Mr Kurtz!" broke the stick of sealing-wax and seemed dumbfounded by the accident. Next thing he wanted to know "how long it would take to" . . . I interrupted him again. Being hungry, you know, and kept on my feet, too, I was getting savage. "How could I tell?" I said. "I hadn't even seen the wreck yet—some months, no doubt." All this talk seemed to me so futile. "Some months," he said. "Well, let us say three months before we can make a start. Yes. That ought to do the affair." I flung out of his hut (he

lived all alone in a clay hut with a sort of veranda) mutter-
ing to myself my opinion of him. He was a chattering
idiot. Afterwards I took it back when it was borne in upon
me startlingly with what extreme nicety he had estimated
the time requisite for the "affair".

'I went to work the next day, turning, so to speak, my
back on that station. In that way only it seemed to me I
could keep my hold on the redeeming facts of life. Still,
one must look about sometimes; and then I saw this
station, these men strolling aimlessly about in the sunshine of the yard. I asked myself sometimes what it all
meant. They wandered here and there with their absurd
long staves in their hands, like a lot of faithless pilgrims
bewitched inside a rotten fence. The word "ivory" rang
in the air, was whispered, was sighed. You would think
they were praying to it. A taint of imbecile rapacity blew
through it all, like a whiff from some corpse. By Jove!
I've never seen anything so unreal in my life. And outside,
the silent wilderness surrounding this cleared speck on
the earth struck me as something great and invincible,
like evil or truth, waiting patiently for the passing away
of this fantastic invasion.

'Oh, these months! Well, never mind. Various things
happened. One evening a grass shed full of calico, cotton
prints, beads, and I don't know what else, burst into a
blaze so suddenly that you would have thought the earth
had opened to let an avenging fire consume all that trash.
I was smoking my pipe quietly by my dismantled steamer,
and saw them all cutting capers in the light, with their
arms lifted high, when the stout man with moustaches
came tearing down to the river, a tin pail in his hand,
assured me that everybody was "behaving splendidly,
splendidly", dipped about a quart of water and tore
back again. I noticed there was a hole in the bottom of
his pail.

'I strolled up. There was no hurry. You see the thing had gone off like a box of matches. It had been hopeless from the very first. The flame had leaped high, driven everybody back, lighted up everything—and collapsed. The shed was already a heap of embers glowing fiercely. A negro was being beaten near by. They said he had caused the fire in some way; be that as it may, he was screeching most horribly. I saw him, later, for several days, sitting in a bit of shade looking very sick and trying to recover himself: afterwards he arose and went out—and the wilderness without a sound took him into its bosom again. As I approached the glow from the dark I found myself at the back of two men, talking. I heard the name of Kurtz pronounced, then the words, "take advantage of this unfortunate accident". One of the men was the manager. I wished him a good evening. "Did you ever see anything like it—eh? It is incredible," he said, and walked off. The other man remained. He was a first-class agent, young, gentlemanly, a bit reserved, with a forked little beard and a hooked nose. He was stand-offish with the other agents, and they on their side said he was the manager's spy upon them. As to me, I had hardly ever spoken to him before. We got into talk, and by and by we strolled away from the hissing ruins. Then he asked me to his room, which was in the main building of the station. He struck a match, and I perceived that this young aristocrat had not only a silver-mounted dressing-case but also a whole candle all to himself. Just at that time the manager was the only man supposed to have any right to candles. Native mats covered the clay walls; a collection of spears, assegais, shields, knives, was hung up in trophies. The business entrusted to this fellow was the making of bricks —so I had been informed; but there wasn't a fragment of a brick anywhere in the station, and he had been there more than a year—waiting. It seems he could not make bricks without something, I don't know what—straw maybe. Anyway, it could not be found there, and as it was not likely to be sent from Europe, it did not appear clear to me what he was waiting for. An act of special creation perhaps. However, they were all waiting—all the sixteen or twenty pilgrims of them—for something; and upon my word it did not seem an uncongenial occupation, from the way they took it, though the only thing that ever came to them was disease—as far as I could see. They beguiled the time by backbiting and intriguing against each other in a foolish kind of way. There was an air of plotting about that station, but nothing came of it, of course. It was as unreal as everything else—as the philanthropic pretence of the whole concern, as their talk, as their government, as their show of work. The only real feeling was a desire to get appointed to a trading-post where ivory was to be had, so that they could earn percentages. They intrigued and slandered and hated each other only on that account—but as to effectually lifting a little finger—oh, no. By heavens! there is something after all in the world allowing one man to steal a horse while another must not look at a halter. Steal a horse straight out. Very well. He has done it. Perhaps he can ride. But there is a way of looking at a halter that would provoke the most charitable of saints into a kick.

'I had no idea why he wanted to be sociable, but as we chatted in there it suddenly occurred to me the fellow was trying to get at something—in fact, pumping me. He alluded constantly to Europe, to the people I was supposed to know there—putting leading questions as to my acquaintances in the sepulchral city, and so on. His little eyes glittered like mica discs—with curiosity—though he tried to keep up a bit of superciliousness. At first I was astonished, but very soon I became awfully curious to see what he would find out from me. I couldn't possibly imagine what I had in me to make it worth his while. It was very pretty to see how he baffled himself, for in truth my body was full only of chills, and my head had nothing in it but that wretched steamboat business. It was evident he took me for a perfectly shameless pre-varicator. At last he got angry, and, to conceal a movement of furious annoyance, he yawned. I rose. Then I noticed a small sketch in oils, on a panel, representing a woman, draped and blindfolded, carrying a lighted torch. The background was sombre—almost black. The movement of the woman was stately, and the effect of the torch-light on the face was sinister.

'It arrested me, and he stood by civilly, holding an empty half-pint champagne bottle (medical comforts) with the candle stuck in it. To my question he said Mr Kurtz had painted this—in this very station more than a year ago—while waiting for means to go to his trading-post. "Tell me, pray," said I, "who is this Mr Kurtz?"

'"The chief of the Inner Station," he answered in a short tone, looking away. "Much obliged," I said, laugh-ing. "And you are the brickmaker of the Central Station. Everyone knows that." He was silent for a while. "He is a prodigy," he said at last. "He is an emissary of pity, and science, and progress, and devil knows what else. We want", he began to declaim suddenly, "for the guidance of the cause entrusted to us by Europe, so to speak, higher intelligence, wide sympathies, a singleness of purpose." "Who says that?" I asked. "Lots of them," he replied. "Some even write that; and so *he* comes here, a special being, as you ought to know." "Why ought I to know?" I interrupted, really surprised. He paid no attention. "Yes. Today he is chief of the best station, next year he will be assistant manager, two years more and . . . but I dare say you know what he will be in two years' time. You are of the new gang—the gang of virtue. The same

c

people who sent him specially also recommended you. Oh, don't say no. I've my own eyes to trust." Light dawned upon me. My dear aunt's influential acquaintances were producing an unexpected effect upon that young man. I nearly burst into a laugh. "Do you read the Company's confidential correspondence?" I asked. He hadn't a word to say. It was great fun. "When Mr Kurtz", I continued, severely, "is General Manager, you won't have the opportunity."

'He blew the candle out suddenly, and we went outside. The moon had risen. Black figures strolled about listlessly, pouring water on the glow, whence proceeded a sound of hissing; steam ascended in the moonlight, the beaten negro groaned somewhere. "What a row the brute makes!" said the indefatigable man with the moustaches, appearing near us. "Serve him right. Transgression— punishment—bang! Pitiless, pitiless. That's the only way. This will prevent all conflagrations for the future. I was just telling the manager . . ." He noticed my companion, and became crestfallen all at once. "Not in bed yet," he said, with a kind of servile heartiness; "it's so natural. Ha! Danger—agitation." He vanished. I went on to the riverside, and the other followed me. I heard a scathing murmur at my ear: "Heap of muffs—go to." The pilgrims could be seen in knots gesticulating, discussing. Several had still their staves in their hands. I verily believe they took these sticks to bed with them. Beyond the fence the forest stood up spectrally in the moonlight, and through the dim stir, through the faint sounds of that lamentable courtyard, the silence of the land went home to one's very heart—its mystery, its greatness, the amazing reality of its concealed life. The hurt negro moaned feebly some- where near by, and then fetched a deep sigh that made me mend my pace away from there. I felt a hand intro- ducing itself under my arm. "My dear sir," said the fellow, "I don't want to be misunderstood, and especially by you, who will see Mr Kurtz long before I can have that pleasure. I wouldn't like him to get a false idea of my disposition. . . ."

'I let him run on, this papier mâché Mephistopheles, and it seemed to me that if I tried I could poke my forefinger through him, and would find nothing inside but a little loose dirt, maybe. He, don't you see, had been planning to be assistant manager by and by under the present man, and I could see that the coming of that Kurtz had upset them both not a little. He talked precipitately, and I did not try to stop him. I had my shoulders against the wreck of my steamer, hauled up on the slope like a carcass of some big river animal. The smell of mud, of primeval mud, by Jove! was in my nostrils, the high stillness of primeval forest was before my eyes; there were shiny patches on the black creek. The moon had spread over everything a thin layer of silver—over the rank grass, over the mud, upon the wall of matted vegetation standing higher than the wall of a temple, over the great river I could see through a sombre gap glittering, glittering, as it flowed broadly by without a murmur. All this was great, expectant, mute, while the man jabbered about himself. I wondered whether the stillness on the face of the immensity looking at us two were meant as an appeal or as a menace. What were we who had strayed in here? Could we handle that dumb thing, or would it handle us? I felt how big, how confoundedly big, was that thing that couldn't talk, and perhaps was deaf as well. What was in there? I could see a little ivory coming out from there, and I had heard Mr Kurtz was in there. I had heard enough about it, too—God knows! Yet somehow it didn't bring any image with it—no more than if I had been told an angel or a fiend was in there. I believed it in the same way one of you might believe there are inhabitants in the planet Mars. I knew once a Scotch sailmaker who was certain, dead sure, there were people in Mars. If you asked him for some idea how they looked and behaved, he would get shy and mutter something about "walking on all fours". If you as much as smiled, he would— though a man of sixty—offer to fight you. I would not have gone so far as to fight for Kurtz, but I went for him near enough to a lie. You know I hate, detest, and can't bear a lie, not because I am straighter than the rest of us, but simply because it appals me. There is a taint of death, a flavour of mortality in lies—which is exactly what I hate and detest in the world—what I want to forget. It makes me miserable and sick, like biting something rotten would do. Temperament, I suppose. Well, I went near enough to it by letting the young fool there believe anything he liked to imagine as to my influence in Europe. I became in an instant as much of a pretence as the rest of the bewitched pilgrims. This simply because I had a notion it somehow would be of help to that Kurtz whom at the time I did not see—you understand. He was just a word for me. I did not see the man in the name any more than you do. Do you see him? Do you see the story? Do you see anything? It seems to me I am trying to tell you a dream—making a vain attempt, because no relation of a dream can convey the dream sensation, that commingling of absurdity, surprise, and bewilderment in a tremor of struggling revolt, that notion of being captured by the incredible which is of the very essence of dreams. . . .'

He was silent for a while.

'. . . No, it is impossible; it is impossible to convey the life sensation of any given epoch of one's existence—that which makes its truth, its meaning—its subtle and penetrating essence. It is impossible. We live, as we dream— alone. . . .'

He paused again as if reflecting, then added:

'Of course in this you fellows see more than I could then. You see me, whom you know. . . .'

It had become so pitch dark that we listeners could hardly see one another. For a long time already he, sitting apart, had been no more to us than a voice. There was not a word from anybody. The others might have been asleep, but I was awake. I listened, I listened on the watch for the sentence, for the word, that would give me the clue to the faint uneasiness inspired by this narrative that seemed to shape itself without human lips in the heavy night air of the river.

'. . . Yes—I let him run on,' Marlow began again, 'and think what he pleased about the powers that were behind me. I did! And there was nothing behind me! There was nothing but that wretched, old, mangled steamboat I was leaning against, while he talked fluently about "the necessity for every man to get on"; "And when one comes out here, you conceive, it is not to gaze at the moon." Mr Kurtz was a "universal genius", but even a genius would find it easier to work with "adequate tools—intelligent men". He did not make bricks—why, there was a physical impossibility in the way—as I was well aware; and if he did secretarial work for the manager, it was because "no sensible man rejects wantonly the confidence of his superiors". Did I see it? I saw it. What more did I want? What I really wanted was rivets, by heaven! Rivets. To get on with the work—to stop the hole. Rivets I wanted. There were cases of them down at the coast—cases—piled up—burst—split! You kicked a loose rivet at every second step in that station yard on the hillside. Rivets had rolled into the grove of death. You could fill your pockets with rivets for the trouble of stooping down—and there wasn't one rivet to be found where it was wanted. We had plates that would do, but nothing to fasten them with. And every week the messenger, a lone negro, letter-bag on

shoulder and staff in hand, left our station for the coast.
And several times a week a coast caravan came in with
trade goods—ghastly glazed calico that made you shudder
only to look at it, glass beads value about a penny a quart,
confounded spotted cotton handkerchiefs. And no rivets.
Three carriers could have brought all that was wanted
to set that steamboat afloat.

'He was becoming confidential now, but I fancy my
unresponsive attitude must have exasperated him at last,
for he judged it necessary to inform me he feared neither
God nor devil, let alone any mere man. I said I could see
that very well, but what I wanted was a certain quantity
of rivets—and rivets were what really Mr Kurtz wanted, if
he had only known it. Now letters went to the coast every
week. . . . "My dear sir," he cried, "I write from dicta-
tion." I demanded rivets. There was a way—for an intelligent man. He changed his manner; became very cold, and
suddenly began to talk about a hippopotamus; wondered
whether sleeping on board the steamer (I stuck to my
salvage night and day) I wasn't disturbed. There was an
old hippo that had the bad habit of getting out on the bank
and roaming at night over the station grounds. The
pilgrims used to turn out in a body and empty every rifle
they could lay hands on at him. Some even had sat up o'
nights for him. All this energy was wasted, though. "That
animal has a charmed life," he said; "but you can say this
only of brutes in this country. No man—you apprehend
me?—no man here bears a charmed life." He stood there
for a moment in the moonlight with his delicate hooked
nose set a little askew, and his mica eyes glittering without
a wink, then, with a curt "Good night", he strode off. I
could see he was disturbed and considerably puzzled,
which made me feel more hopeful than I had been for
days. It was a great comfort to turn from that chap to my
influential friend, the battered, twisted, ruined, tin-pot

steamboat. I clambered on board. She rang under my feet like an empty Huntley & Palmer biscuit tin kicked along a gutter; she was nothing so solid in make, and rather less pretty in shape, but I had expended enough hard work on her to make me love her. No influential friend would have served me better. She had given me a chance to come out a bit—to find out what I could do. No, I don't like work. I had rather laze about and think of all the fine things that can be done. I don't like work— no man does—but I like what is in the work—the chance to find yourself. Your own reality—for yourself, not for others—what no other man can ever know. They can only see the mere show, and never can tell what it really means.

'I was not surprised to see somebody sitting aft, on the deck, with his legs dangling over the mud. You see I rather chummed with the few mechanics there were in that station, whom the other pilgrims naturally despised —on account of their imperfect manners, I suppose. This was the foreman—a boiler-maker by trade—a good worker. He was a lank, bony, yellow-faced man, with big intense eyes. His aspect was worried, and his head was as bald as the palm of my hand; but his hair in falling seemed to have stuck to his chin, and had prospered in the new locality, for his beard hung down to his waist. He was a widower with six young children (he had left them in charge of a sister of his to come out there), and the passion of his life was pigeon-flying. He was an enthu- siast and a connoisseur. He would rave about pigeons. After work hours he used sometimes to come over from his hut for a talk about his children and his pigeons; at work, when he had to crawl in the mud under the bottom of the steamboat, he would tie up that beard of his in a kind of white serviette he brought for the purpose. It had loops to go over his ears. In the evening he could be seen squatted on the bank rinsing that wrapper in the creek with great care, then spreading it solemnly on a bush to dry.

'I slapped him on the back and shouted: "We shall have rivets!" He scrambled to his feet exclaiming, "No! Rivets!" as though he couldn't believe his ears. Then in a low voice: "You ... eh?" I don't know why we behaved like lunatics. I put my finger to the side of my nose and nodded mysteriously. "Good for you!" he cried, snapped his fingers above his head, lifting one foot. I tried a jig. We capered on the iron deck. A frightful clatter came out of that hulk, and the virgin forest on the other bank of the creek sent it back in a thundering roll upon the sleeping station. It must have made some of the pilgrims sit up in their hovels. A dark figure obscured the lighted doorway of the manager's hut, vanished, then, a second or so after, the doorway itself vanished, too. We stopped, and the silence driven away by the stamping of our feet flowed back again from the recesses of the land. The great wall of vegetation, an exuberant and entangled mass of trunks, branches, leaves, boughs, festoons, motionless in the moonlight, was like a rioting invasion of soundless life, a rolling wave of plants, piled up, crested, ready to topple over the creek, to sweep every little man of us out of his little existence. And it moved not. A deadened burst of mighty splashes and snorts reached us from afar, as though an ichthyosaurus had been taking a bath of glitter in the great river. "After all," said the boiler-maker in a reasonable tone, "why shouldn't we get the rivets?" Why not, indeed! I did not know of any reason why we shouldn't. "They'll come in three weeks," I said confidently.

'But they didn't. Instead of rivets there came an invasion, an infliction, a visitation. It came in sections during the next three weeks, each section headed by a donkey carrying a white man in new clothes and tan shoes, bowing from that elevation right and left to the impressed pilgrims.

A quarrelsome band of footsore sulky negroes trod on the heels of the donkey; a lot of tents, camp-stools, tin boxes, white cases, brown bales, would be shot down in the court-yard, and the air of mystery would deepen a little over the muddle of the station. Five such instalments came, with their absurd air of disorderly flight with the loot of in-numerable outfit shops and provision stores, that, one would think, they were lugging, after a raid, into the wilderness for equitable division. It was an inextricable mess of things decent in themselves but that human folly made look like spoils of thieving.

'This devoted band called itself the Eldorado Exploring Expedition, and I believe they were sworn to secrecy. Their talk, however, was the talk of sordid buccaneers: it was reckless without hardihood, greedy without audacity, and cruel without courage; there was not an atom of foresight or of serious intention in the whole batch of them, and they did not seem aware these things are wanted for the work of the world. To tear treasure out of the bowels of the land was their desire, with no more moral purpose at the back of it than there is in burglars breaking into a safe. Who paid the expenses of the noble enterprise I don't know; but the uncle of our manager was leader of that lot.

'In exterior he resembled a butcher in a poor neigh-bourhood, and his eyes had a look of sleepy cunning. He carried his fat paunch with ostentation on his short legs, and during the time his gang infested the station spoke to no one but his nephew. You could see these two roaming about all day long with their heads close together in an everlasting confab.

'I had given up worrying myself about the rivets. One's capacity for that kind of folly is more limited than you would suppose. I said "Hang!"—and let things slide. I had plenty of time for meditation, and now and then I

* C

would give some thought to Kurtz. I wasn't very interested in him. No. Still, I was curious to see whether this man, who had come out equipped with moral ideas of some sort, would climb to the top after all and how he would set about his work when there.'

II

'One evening as I was lying flat on the deck of my steamboat, I heard voices approaching—and there were the nephew and the uncle strolling along the bank. I laid my head on my arm again, and had nearly lost myself in a doze, when somebody said in my ear, as it were: "I am as harmless as a little child, but I don't like to be dictated to. Am I the manager—or am I not? I was ordered to send him there. It's incredible." . . . I became aware that the two were standing on the shore alongside the forepart of the steamboat, just below my head. I did not move; it did not occur to me to move: I was sleepy. "It *is* unpleasant," grunted the uncle. "He has asked the Administration to be sent there", said the other, "with the idea of showing what he could do; and I was instructed accordingly. Look at the influence that man must have. Is it not frightful?" They both agreed it was frightful, then made several bizarre remarks: "Make rain and fine weather—one man—the Council—by the nose"—bits of absurd sentences that got the better of my drowsiness, so that I had pretty near the whole of my wits about me when the uncle said, "The climate may do away with this difficulty for you. Is he alone there?" "Yes," answered the manager; "he sent his assistant down the river with a note to me in these terms: 'Clear this poor devil out of the country, and don't bother sending more of that sort. I had rather be alone than have the kind of men you can dispose of with me.' It was more than a year ago. Can you imagine such impudence!" "Anything since then?" asked the other, hoarsely. "Ivory," jerked the nephew; "lots of it—prime sort—lots—most annoying, from him." "And with that?" questioned the heavy rumble. "Invoice," was the reply fired out, so to speak. Then silence. They had been talking about Kurtz.

'I was broad awake by this time, but, lying perfectly at ease, remained still, having no inducement to change my position. "How did that ivory come all this way?" growled the elder man, who seemed very vexed. The other explained that it had come with a fleet of canoes in charge of an English half-caste clerk Kurtz had with him; that Kurtz had apparently intended to return himself, the station being by that time bare of goods and stores, but after coming three hundred miles, had suddenly decided to go back, which he started to do alone in a small dugout with four paddlers, leaving the half-caste to continue down the river with the ivory. The two fellows there seemed astounded at anybody attempting such a thing. They were at a loss for an adequate motive. As to me, I seemed to see Kurtz for the first time. It was a distinct glimpse: the dugout, four paddling savages, and the lone white man turning his back suddenly on the headquarters, on relief, on thoughts of home—perhaps; setting his face towards the depths of the wilderness; towards his empty and desolate station. I did not know the motive. Perhaps he was just simply a fine fellow who stuck to his work for its own sake. His name, you understand, had not been pronounced once. He was "that man". The half-caste, who, as far as I could see, had conducted a difficult trip with great prudence and pluck, was invariably alluded to as "that scoundrel". The "scoundrel" had reported that the "man" had been very ill—had recovered imperfectly. . . . The two below me moved away then a few paces, and strolled back and forth at some little distance. I heard: "Military post—doctor—two hundred miles—quite alone now—unavoidable delays—nine months—no news—strange rumours." They approached again, just as the manager was saying: "No one, as far as I know, unless a species of wandering trader—a pestilential fellow, snapping ivory from the natives." Who was it they were talking about now? I gathered in snatches that this was some man supposed to be in Kurtz's district, and of whom the manager did not approve. "We will not be free from unfair competition till one of these fellows is hanged for an example," he said. "Certainly," grunted the other; "get him hanged! Why not? Anything— anything can be done in this country. That's what I say; nobody here, you understand, *here*, can endanger your position. And why? You stand the climate—you outlast them all. The danger is in Europe; but there before I left I took care to . . ." They moved off and whispered, then their voices rose again. "The extraordinary series of delays is not my fault. I did my best." The fat man sighed. "Very sad." "And the pestiferous absurdity of his talk," continued the other; "he bothered me enough when he was here. 'Each station should be like a beacon on the road towards better things, a centre for trade of course, but also for humanizing, improving, instructing.' Conceive you— that ass! And he wants to be manager! No, it's——" Here he got choked by excessive indignation, and I lifted my head the least bit. I was surprised to see how near they were—right under me. I could have spat upon their hats. They were looking on the ground, absorbed in thought. The manager was switching his leg with a slender twig: his sagacious relative lifted his head. "You have been well since you came out this time?" he asked. The other gave a start. "Who? I? Oh, like a charm—like a charm! But the rest—oh, my goodness! All sick. They die so quick, too, that I haven't the time to send them out of the country —it's incredible!" "H'm. Just so," grunted the uncle. "Ah, my boy, trust to this—I say, trust to this." I saw him extend his short flipper of an arm for a gesture that took in the forest, the creek, the mud, the river—seemed to beckon with a dishonouring flourish before the sunlit face of the land a treacherous appeal to the lurking death, to the hidden evil, to the profound darkness of its heart. It was so startling that I leaped to my feet and looked back at the edge of the forest, as though I had expected an answer of some sort to that black display of confidence. You know the foolish notions that come to one sometimes. The high stillness confronted these two figures with its ominous patience, waiting for the passing away of a fantastic invasion.

'They swore aloud together—out of sheer fright, I believe—then, pretending not to know anything of my existence, turned back to the station. The sun was low; and leaning forward side by side, they seemed to be tugging painfully uphill their two ridiculous shadows of unequal length, that trailed behind them slowly over the tall grass without bending a single blade.

'In a few days the Eldorado Expedition went into the patient wilderness, that closed upon it as the sea closes over a diver. Long afterwards the news came that all the donkeys were dead. I know nothing as to the fate of the less valuable animals. They, no doubt, like the rest of us, found what they deserved. I did not inquire. I was then rather excited at the prospect of meeting Kurtz very soon. When I say very soon I mean it comparatively. It was just two months from the day we left the creek when we came to the bank below Kurtz's station.

'Going up that river was like travelling back to the earliest beginnings of the world, when vegetation rioted

on the earth and the big trees were kings. An empty
stream, a great silence, an impenetrable forest. The air
was warm, thick, heavy, sluggish. There was no joy in the
brilliance of sunshine. The long stretches of the waterway
ran on, deserted, into the gloom of overshadowed distances. On silvery sandbanks hippos and alligators sunned
themselves side by side. The broadening waters flowed
through a mob of wooded islands; you lost your way on
that river as you would in a desert, and butted all day
long against shoals, trying to find the channel, till you
thought yourself bewitched and cut off for ever from everything you had known once—somewhere—far away—in
another existence perhaps. There were moments when
one's past came back to one, as it will sometimes when you
have not a moment to spare to yourself; but it came in the
shape of an unrestful and noisy dream, remembered with
wonder amongst the overwhelming realities of this strange
world of plants, and water, and silence. And this stillness
of life did not in the least resemble a peace. It was the
stillness of an implacable force brooding over an inscrutable intention. It looked at you with a vengeful aspect. I
got used to it afterwards; I did not see it any more; I had
no time. I had to keep guessing at the channel; I had to
discern, mostly by inspiration, the signs of hidden banks;
I watched for sunken stones; I was learning to clap my
teeth smartly before my heart flew out, when I shaved by
a fluke some infernal sly old snag that would have ripped
the life out of the tin-pot steamboat and drowned all the
pilgrims; I had to keep a look-out for the signs of dead
wood we could cut up in the night for next day's steaming.
When you have to attend to things of that sort, to the
mere incidents of the surface, the reality—the reality, I
tell you—fades. The inner truth is hidden—luckily,
luckily. But I felt it all the same; I felt often its mysterious
stillness watching me at my monkey tricks, just as it

watches you fellows performing on your respective tight-ropes for—what is it?—half a crown a tumble——'

'Try to be civil, Marlow,' growled a voice, and I knew there was at least one listener awake besides myself.

'I beg your pardon. I forgot the heartache which makes up the rest of the price. And indeed what does the price matter, if the trick be well done? You do your tricks very well. And I didn't do badly either, since I managed not to sink that steamboat on my first trip. It's a wonder to me yet. Imagine a blindfolded man set to drive a van over a bad road. I sweated and shivered over that business considerably, I can tell you. After all, for a seaman, to scrape the bottom of the thing that's supposed to float all the time under his care is the unpardonable sin. No one may know of it, but you never forget the thump—eh? A blow on the very heart. You remember it, you dream of it, you wake up at night and think of it—years after—and go hot and cold all over. I don't pretend to say that steamboat floated all the time. More than once she had to wade for a bit, with twenty cannibals splashing around and pushing. We had enlisted some of these chaps on the way for a crew. Fine fellows—cannibals—in their place. They were men one could work with, and I am grateful to them. And, after all, they did not eat each other before my face: they had brought along a provision of hippo meat which went rotten, and made the mystery of the wilderness stink in my nostrils. Phoo! I can sniff it now. I had the manager on board and three or four pilgrims with their staves—all complete. Sometimes we came upon a station close by the bank, clinging to the skirts of the unknown, and the white men rushing out of a tumble-down hovel, with great gestures of joy and surprise and welcome, seemed very strange—had the appearance of being held there captive by a spell. The word ivory would ring in the air for a while—and on we went again into the

greed

silence, along empty reaches, round the still bends, between the high walls of our winding way, reverberating in hollow claps the ponderous beat of the stern-wheel. Trees, trees, millions of trees, massive, immense, running up high; and at their foot, hugging the bank against the stream, crept the little begrimed steamboat, like a sluggish beetle crawling on the floor of a lofty portico. It made you feel very small, very lost, and yet it was not altogether depressing, that feeling. After all, if you were small, the grimy beetle crawled on—which was just what you wanted it to do. Where the pilgrims imagined it crawled to I don't know. To some place where they expected to get something, I bet! For me it crawled towards Kurtz—exclusively; but when the steam-pipes started leaking we crawled very slow. The reaches opened before us and closed behind, as if the forest had stepped leisurely across the water to bar the way for our return. We penetrated deeper and deeper into the heart of darkness. It was very quiet there. At night sometimes the roll of drums behind the curtain of trees would run up the river and remain sustained faintly, as if hovering in the air high over our heads, till the first break of day. Whether it meant war, peace, or prayer we could not tell. The dawns were heralded by the descent of a chill stillness; the woodcutters slept, their fires burned low; the snapping of a twig would make you start. We were wanderers on prehistoric earth, on an earth that wore the aspect of an unknown planet. We could have fancied ourselves the first of men taking possession of an accursed inheritance, to be subdued at the cost of profound anguish and of excessive toil. But suddenly, as we struggled round a bend, there would be a glimpse of rush walls, of peaked grass roofs, a burst of yells, a whirl of black limbs, a mass of hands clapping, of feet stamping, of bodies swaying, of eyes rolling, under the droop of heavy and motionless foliage. The steamer toiled along slowly on the edge of a black and incomprehensible frenzy. The prehistoric man was cursing us, praying to us, welcoming us—who could tell? We were cut off from the comprehension of our surroundings; we glided past like phantoms, wondering and secretly appalled, as sane men would be before an enthusiastic outbreak in a madhouse. We could not understand because we were too far and could not remember, because we were travelling in the night of first ages, of those ages that are gone, leaving hardly a sign—and no memories.

'The earth seemed unearthly. We are accustomed to look upon the shackled form of a conquered monster, but there—there you could look at a thing monstrous and free. It was unearthly, and the men were—— No, they were not inhuman. Well, you know, that was the worst of it—this suspicion of their not being inhuman. It would come slowly to one. They howled and leaped, and spun, and made horrid faces; but what thrilled you was just the thought of their humanity—like yours—the thought of your remote kinship with this wild and passionate uproar. Ugly. Yes, it was ugly enough; but if you were man enough you would admit to yourself that there was in you just the faintest trace of a response to the terrible frankness of that noise, a dim suspicion of there being a meaning in it which you—you so remote from the night of first ages—could comprehend. And why not? The mind of man is capable of anything—because everything is in it, all the past as well as all the future. What was there after all? Joy, fear, sorrow, devotion, valour, rage—who can tell?—but truth—truth stripped of its cloak of time. Let the fool gape and shudder—the man knows, and can look on without a wink. But he must at least be as much of a man as these on the shore. He must meet that truth with his own true stuff—with his own inborn strength.

Principles won't do. Acquisitions, clothes, pretty rags—
rags that would fly off at the first good shake. No; you
want a deliberate belief. An appeal to me in this fiendish
row—is there? Very well; I hear; I admit, but I have a
voice, too, and for good or evil mine is the speech that cannot be silenced. Of course, a fool, what with sheer fright
and fine sentiments, is always safe. Who's that grunting?
You wonder I didn't go ashore for a howl and a dance?
Well, no—I didn't. Fine sentiments, you say? Fine sentiments, be hanged! I had no time. I had to mess about with
white-lead and strips of woollen blanket helping to put band-
ages on those leaky steam-pipes—I tell you. I had to watch
the steering, and circumvent those snags, and get the tin-
pot along by hook or by crook. There was surface-truth
enough in these things to save a wiser man. And between
whiles I had to look after the savage who was fireman.
He was an improved specimen; he could fire up a vertical
boiler. He was there below me, and, upon my word, to
look at him was as edifying as seeing a dog in a parody of
breeches and a feather hat, walking on his hind-legs. A
few months of training had done for that really fine chap.
He squinted at the steam-gauge and at the water-gauge
with an evident effort of intrepidity—and he had filed
teeth, too, the poor devil, and the wool of his pate shaved
into queer patterns, and three ornamental scars on each
of his cheeks. He ought to have been clapping his hands
and stamping his feet on the bank, instead of which he
was hard at work, a thrall to strange witchcraft, full of
improving knowledge. He was useful because he had been
instructed; and what he knew was this—that should the
water in that transparent thing disappear, the evil spirit
inside the boiler would get angry through the greatness
of his thirst, and take a terrible vengeance. So he sweated
and fired up and watched the glass fearfully (with an
impromptu charm, made of rags, tied to his arm, and a

piece of polished bone, as big as a watch, stuck flatways through his lower lip), while the wooded banks slipped past us slowly, the short noise was left behind, the interminable miles of silence—and we crept on, towards Kurtz. But the snags were thick, the water was treacherous and shallow, the boiler seemed indeed to have a sulky devil in it, and thus neither that fireman nor I had any time to peer into our creepy thoughts.

'Some fifty miles below the Inner Station we came upon a hut of reeds, an inclined and melancholy pole, with the unrecognizable tatters of what had been a flag of some sort flying from it, and a neatly stacked wood-pile. This was unexpected. We came to the bank, and on the stack of firewood found a flat piece of board with some faded pencil writing on it. When deciphered it said: "Wood for you. Hurry up. Approach cautiously." There was a signature, but it was illegible—not Kurtz—a much longer word. Hurry up. Where? Up the river? "Approach cautiously." We had not done so. But the warning could not have been meant for the place where it could be only found after approach. Something was wrong above. But what—and how much? That was the question. We commented adversely upon the imbecility of that telegraphic style. The bush around said nothing, and would not let us look very far, either. A torn curtain of red twill hung in the doorway of the hut, and flapped sadly in our faces. The dwelling was dismantled; but we could see a white man had lived there not very long ago. There remained a rude table—a plank on two posts; a heap of rubbish reposed in a dark corner, and by the door I picked up a book. It had lost its covers, and the pages had been thumbed into a state of extremely dirty softness; but the back had been lovingly stitched afresh with white cotton thread, which looked clean yet. It was an extraordinary find. Its title was, *An Inquiry into some Points of Seamanship*, by a man Tower, Towson—some such name—Master in His Majesty's Navy. The matter looked dreary reading enough, with illustrative diagrams and repulsive tables of figures, and the copy was sixty years old. I handled this amazing antiquity with the greatest possible tenderness, lest it should dissolve in my hands. Within, Towson or Towser was inquiring earnestly into the breaking strain of ships' chains and tackle, and other such matters. Not a very enthralling book; but at the first glance you could see there a singleness of intention, an honest concern for the right way of going to work, which made these humble pages, thought out so many years ago, luminous with another than a professional light. The simple old sailor, with his talk of chains and purchases, made me forget the jungle and the pilgrims in a delicious sensation of having come upon something unmistakably real. Such a book being there was wonderful enough; but still more astounding were the notes pencilled in the margin, and plainly referring to the text. I couldn't believe my eyes! They were in cipher! Yes, it looked like cipher. Fancy a man lugging with him a book of that description into this nowhere and studying it—and making notes—in cipher at that! It was an extravagant mystery.

'I had been dimly aware for some time of a worrying noise, and when I lifted my eyes I saw the wood-pile was gone, and the manager, aided by all the pilgrims, was shouting at me from the riverside. I slipped the book into my pocket. I assure you to leave off reading was like tearin ; myself away from the shelter of an old and solid friendship.

'I started the lame engine ahead. "It must be this miserable trader—this intruder," exclaimed the manager, looking back malevolently at the place we had left. "He must be English," I said. "It will not save him from getting into trouble if he is not careful," muttered the manager darkly. I observed with assumed innocence that no man was safe from trouble in this world.

'The current was more rapid now, the steamer seemed at her last gasp, the stern-wheel flopped languidly, and I caught myself listening on tiptoe for the next beat of the boat, for in sober truth I expected the wretched thing to give up every moment. It was like watching the last flickers of a life. But still we crawled. Sometimes I would pick out a tree a little way ahead to measure our progress towards Kurtz by, but I lost it invariably before we got abreast. To keep the eyes so long on one thing was too much for human patience. The manager displayed a beautiful resignation. I fretted and fumed and took to arguing with myself whether or no I would talk openly with Kurtz; but before I could come to any conclusion it occurred to me that my speech or my silence, indeed any action of mine, would be a mere futility. What did it matter what anyone knew or ignored? What did it matter who was manager? One gets sometimes such a flash of insight. The essentials of this affair lay deep under the surface, beyond my reach, and beyond my power of meddling.

'Towards the evening of the second day we judged ourselves about eight miles from Kurtz's station. I wanted to push on; but the manager looked grave, and told me the navigation up there was so dangerous that it would be advisable, the sun being very low already, to wait where we were till next morning. Moreover, he pointed out that if the warning to approach cautiously were to be followed, we must approach in daylight—not at dusk, or in the dark. This was sensible enough. Eight miles meant nearly three hours' steaming for us, and I could also see suspicious ripples at the upper end of the reach. Nevertheless, I was annoyed beyond expression at the delay, and most unreasonably, too, since one night more

could not matter much after so many months. As we had
plenty of wood, and caution was the word, I brought up
in the middle of the stream. The reach was narrow,
straight, with high sides like a railway cutting. The dusk
came gliding into it long before the sun had set. The current ran smooth and swift, but a dumb immobility sat on
the banks. The living trees, lashed together by the creepers
and every living bush of the undergrowth, might have been
changed into stone, even to the slenderest twig, to the
lightest leaf. It was not sleep—it seemed unnatural, like a
state of trance. Not the faintest sound of any kind could
be heard. You looked on amazed, and began to suspect
yourself of being deaf—then the night came suddenly,
and struck you blind as well. About three in the morning
some large fish leaped, and the loud splash made me jump
as though a gun had been fired. When the sun rose there
was a white fog, very warm and clammy, and more
blinding than the night. It did not shift or drive; it was
just there, standing all round you like something solid.
At eight or nine, perhaps, it lifted as a shutter lifts. We
had a glimpse of the towering multitude of trees, of the
immense matted jungle, with the blazing little ball of the
sun hanging over it—all perfectly still—and then the
white shutter came down again, smoothly, as if sliding in
greased grooves. I ordered the chain, which we had begun
to heave in, to be paid out again. Before it stopped running
with a muffled rattle, a cry, a very loud cry, as of infinite
desolation, soared slowly in the opaque air. It ceased. A
complaining clamour, modulated in savage discords,
filled our ears. The sheer unexpectedness of it made my
hair stir under my cap. I don't know how it struck the
others: to me it seemed as though the mist itself had
screamed, so suddenly, and apparently from all sides at
once, did this tumultuous and mournful uproar arise.
It culminated in a hurried outbreak of almost intolerably

excessive shrieking, which stopped short, leaving us stiffened in a variety of silly attitudes, and obstinately listening
to the nearly as appalling and excessive silence. "Good
God! What is the meaning——" stammered at my elbow
one of the pilgrims, a little fat man, with sandy hair and
red whiskers, who wore side-spring boots, and pink
pyjamas tucked into his socks. Two others remained open-
mouthed a whole minute, then dashed into the little cabin,
to rush out incontinently and stand darting scared glances,
with Winchesters at "ready" in their hands. What we
could see was just the steamer we were on, her outlines
blurred as though she had been on the point of dissolving,
and a misty strip of water, perhaps two feet broad, around
her—and that was all. The rest of the world was nowhere,
as far as our eyes and ears were concerned. Just nowhere.
Gone, disappeared; swept off without leaving a whisper
or a shadow behind.

'I went forward, and ordered the chain to be hauled
in short, so as to be ready to trip the anchor and move
the steamboat at once if necessary. "Will they attack?"
whispered an awed voice. "We will be all butchered in
this fog," murmured another. The faces twitched with the
strain, the hands trembled slightly, the eyes forgot to wink.
It was very curious to see the contrast of expressions of the
white men and of the black fellows of our crew, who were
as much strangers to that part of the river as we, though
their homes were only eight hundred miles away. The
whites, of course greatly discomposed, had besides a
curious look of being painfully shocked by such an outrageous row. The others had an alert, naturally interested
expression; but their faces were essentially quiet, even
those of the one or two who grinned as they hauled at the
chain. Several exchanged short, grunting phrases, which
seemed to settle the matter to their satisfaction. Their
headman, a young, broad-chested black, severely draped

in dark-blue fringed cloths, with fierce nostrils and his hair all done up artfully in oily ringlets, stood near me. "Aha!" I said, just for good fellowship's sake. "Catch 'im," he snapped, with a bloodshot widening of his eyes and a flash of sharp teeth, "catch 'im. Give 'im to us." "To you, eh?" I asked. "What would you do with them?" "Eat 'im!" he said, curtly, and, leaning his elbow on the rail, looked out into the fog in a dignified and profoundly pensive attitude. I would no doubt have been properly horrified, had it not occurred to me that he and his chaps must be very hungry: that they must have been growing increasingly hungry for at least this month past. They had been engaged for six months (I don't think a single one of them had any clear idea of time, as we at the end of countless ages have. They still belonged to the beginnings of time—had no inherited experience to teach them as it were), and of course, as long as there was a piece of paper written over in accordance with some farcical law or other made down the river, it didn't enter anybody's head to trouble how they would live. Certainly they had brought with them some rotten hippo meat, which couldn't have lasted very long, anyway, even if the pilgrims hadn't, in the midst of a shocking hullabaloo, thrown a considerable quantity of it overboard. It looked like a high-handed proceeding; but it was really a case of legitimate self-defence. You can't breathe dead hippo waking, sleeping, and eating, and at the same time keep your precarious grip on existence. Besides that, they had given them every week three pieces of brass wire, each about nine inches long; and the theory was they were to buy their provisions with that currency in riverside villages. You can see how *that* worked. There were either no villages, or the people were hostile, or the director, who like the rest of us fed out of tins, with an occasional old he-goat thrown in, didn't want to stop the steamer for some more or less recondite reason. So, unless they swallowed the wire itself, or made loops of it to snare the fishes with, I don't see what good their extravagant salary could be to them. I must say it was paid with a regularity worthy of a large and honourable trading company. For the rest, the only thing to eat —though it didn't look eatable in the least—I saw in their possession was a few lumps of some stuff like half-cooked dough, of a dirty lavender colour, they kept wrapped in leaves, and now and then swallowed a piece of, but so small that it seemed done more for the looks of the thing than for any serious purpose of sustenance. Why in the name of all the gnawing devils of hunger they didn't go for us—they were thirty to five—and have a good tuck in for once, amazes me now when I think of it. They were big powerful men, with not much capacity to weigh the consequences, with courage, with strength, even yet, though their skins were no longer glossy and their muscles no longer hard. And I saw that something restraining, one of those human secrets that baffle probability, had come into play there. I looked at them with a swift quickening of interest—not because it occurred to me I might be eaten by them before very long, though I own to you that just then I perceived—in a new light, as it were—how unwholesome the pilgrims looked, and I hoped, yes, I positively hoped, that my aspect was not so—what shall I say?—so—unappetizing: a touch of fantastic vanity which fitted well with the dream sensation that pervaded all my days at that time. Perhaps I had a little fever, too. One can't live with one's finger everlastingly on one's pulse. I had often "a little fever", or a little touch of other things—the playful paw-strokes of the wilderness, the preliminary trifling before the more serious onslaught which came in due course. Yes; I looked at them as you would on any human being, with a curiosity of their impulses, motives, capacities, weaknesses, when brought

to the test of an inexorable physical necessity. Restraint!
What possible restraint? Was it superstition, disgust,
patience, fear—or some kind of primitive honour? No
fear can stand up to hunger, no patience can wear it out,
disgust simply does not exist where hunger is; and as to
superstition, beliefs, and what you may call principles,
they are less than chaff in a breeze. Don't you know the
devilry of lingering starvation, its exasperating torment,
its black thoughts, its sombre and brooding ferocity? Well,
I do. It takes a man all his inborn strength to fight hunger
properly. It's really easier to face bereavement, dishonour,
and the perdition of one's soul—than this kind of prolonged hunger. Sad, but true. And these chaps, too, had
no earthly reason for any kind of scruple. Restraint! I
would just as soon have expected restraint from a hyena
prowling amongst the corpses of a battlefield. But there
was the fact facing me—the fact dazzling, to be seen, like
the foam on the depths of the sea, like a ripple on an
unfathomable enigma, a mystery greater—when I thought
of it—than the curious, inexplicable note of desperate
grief in this savage clamour that had swept by us on the
river-bank, behind the blind whiteness of the fog.

'Two pilgrims were quarrelling in hurried whispers as
to which bank. "Left." "No, no; how can you? Right,
right, of course." "It is very serious," said the manager's
voice behind me; "I would be desolated if anything should
happen to Mr Kurtz before we came up." I looked at him,
and had not the slightest doubt he was sincere. He was
just the kind of man who would wish to preserve appearances. That was his restraint. But when he muttered
something about going on at once, I did not even take the
trouble to answer him. I knew, and he knew, that it was
impossible. Were we to let go our hold of the bottom, we
would be absolutely in the air—in space. We wouldn't be
able to tell where we were going to—whether up- or

downstream, or across—till we fetched against one bank
or the other—and then we wouldn't know at first which
it was. Of course I made no move. I had no mind for a
smash-up. You couldn't imagine a more deadly place for
a shipwreck. Whether drowned at once or not, we were
sure to perish speedily in one way or another. "I authorize
you to take all the risks," he said, after a short silence. "I
refuse to take any," I said, shortly; which was just the
answer he expected, though its tone might have surprised
him. "Well, I must defer to your judgment. You are captain," he said, with marked civility. I turned my shoulder
to him in sign of my appreciation, and looked into the fog.
How long would it last? It was the most hopeless look-
out. The approach to this Kurtz grubbing for ivory in
the wretched bush was beset by as many dangers as
though he had been an enchanted princess sleeping in
a fabulous castle. "Will they attack, do you think?"
asked the manager, in a confidential tone.

'I did not think they would attack, for several obvious
reasons. The thick fog was one. If they left the bank in
their canoes, they would get lost in it, as we would be if we
attempted to move. Still, I had also judged the jungle of
both banks quite impenetrable—and yet eyes were in it,
eyes that had seen us. The riverside bushes were certainly
very thick; but the undergrowth behind was evidently
penetrable. However, during the short lift I had seen no
canoes anywhere in the reach—certainly not abreast of
the steamer. But what made the idea of attack inconceivable to me was the nature of the noise—of the cries we
had heard. They had not the fierce character boding of
immediate hostile intention. Unexpected, wild, and violent
as they had been, they had given me an irresistible impression of sorrow. The glimpse of the steamboat had for some
reason filled those savages with unrestrained grief. The
danger, if any, I expounded, was from our proximity to a

great human passion let loose. Even extreme grief may
ultimately vent itself in violence—but more generally
takes the form of apathy. . . .

'You should have seen the pilgrims stare! They had
no heart to grin, or even to revile me: but I believe they
thought me gone mad—with fright, maybe. I delivered
a regular lecture. My dear boys, it was no good bothering.
Keep a look-out? Well, you may guess I watched the fog
for the signs of lifting as a cat watches a mouse; but for
anything else our eyes were of no more use to us than if
we had been buried miles deep in a heap of cotton-wool.
It felt like it, too—choking, warm, stifling. Besides, all I
said, though it sounded extravagant, was absolutely true
to fact. What we afterwards alluded to as an attack was
really an attempt at repulse. The action was very far from
being aggressive—it was not even defensive, in the usual
sense: it was undertaken under the stress of desperation,
and in its essence was purely protective.

'It developed itself, I should say, two hours after the
fog lifted, and its commencement was at a spot, roughly
speaking, about a mile and a half below Kurtz's station.
We had just floundered and flopped round a bend, when
I saw an islet, a mere grassy hummock of bright green,
in the middle of the stream. It was the only thing of the
kind; but as we opened the reach more, I perceived it was
the head of a long sandbank, or rather of a chain of shallow
patches stretching down the middle of the river. They
were discoloured, just awash, and the whole lot was seen
just under the water, exactly as a man's backbone is seen
running down the middle of his back under the skin. Now,
as far as I did see, I could go to the right or to the left of
this. I didn't know either channel, of course. The banks
looked pretty well alike, the depth appeared the same;
but as I had been informed the station was on the west
side, I naturally headed for the western passage.

'No sooner had we fairly entered it than I became aware it was much narrower than I had supposed. To the left of us there was the long uninterrupted shoal, and to the right a high, steep bank heavily overgrown with bushes. Above the bush the trees stood in serried ranks. The twigs overhung the current thickly, and from distance to distance a large limb of some tree projected rigidly over the stream. It was then well on in the afternoon, the face of the forest was gloomy, and a broad strip of shadow had already fallen on the water. In this shadow we steamed up—very slowly, as you may imagine. I sheered her well inshore— the water being deepest near the bank, as the sounding-pole informed me.

'One of my hungry and forbearing friends was sounding in the bows just below me. This steamboat was exactly like a decked scow. On the deck there were two little teak-wood houses, with doors and windows. The boiler was in the fore-end, and the machinery right astern. Over the whole there was a light roof, supported on stanchions. The funnel projected through that roof, and in front of the funnel a small cabin built of light planks served for a pilot-house. It contained a couch, two camp-stools, a loaded Martini-Henry leaning in one corner, a tiny table, and the steering-wheel. It had a wide door in front and a broad shutter at each side. All these were always thrown open, of course. I spent my days perched up there on the extreme fore-end of that roof, before the door. At night I slept, or tried to, on the couch. An athletic black belonging to some coast tribe, and educated by my poor predecessor, was the helmsman. He sported a pair of brass earrings, wore a blue cloth wrapper from the waist to the ankles, and thought all the world of himself. He was the most unstable kind of fool I had ever seen. He steered with no end of a swagger while you were by; but if he lost sight of you, he became instantly the prey of an abject funk, and would let that cripple of a steamboat get the upper hand of him in a minute.

'I was looking down at the sounding-pole, and feeling much annoyed to see at each try a little more of it stick out of that river, when I saw my poleman give up the business suddenly, and stretch himself flat on the deck, without even taking the trouble to haul his pole in. He kept hold on it though, and it trailed in the water. At the same time the fireman, whom I could also see below me, sat down abruptly before his furnace and ducked his head. I was amazed. Then I had to look at the river mighty quick, because there was a snag in the fairway. Sticks, little sticks, were flying about—thick: they were whizzing before my nose, dropping below me, striking behind me against my pilot-house. All this time the river, the shore, the woods, were very quiet—perfectly quiet. I could only hear the heavy splashing thump of the stern-wheel and the patter of these things. We cleared the snag clumsily. Arrows, by Jove! We were being shot at! I stepped in quickly to close the shutter on the land side. That fool helmsman, his hands on the spokes, was lifting his knees high, stamping his feet, champing his mouth, like a reined-in horse. Confound him! And we were staggering within ten feet of the bank. I had to lean right out to swing the heavy shutter, and I saw a face amongst the leaves on the level with my own, looking at me very fierce and steady; and then suddenly, as though a veil had been removed from my eyes, I made out, deep in the tangled gloom, naked breasts, arms, legs, glaring eyes—the bush was swarming with human limbs in movement, glistening, of bronze colour. The twigs shook, swayed, and rustled, the arrows flew out of them, and then the shutter came to. "Steer her straight!" I said to the helmsman. He held his head rigid, face forward; but his eyes rolled, he kept on, lifting and setting down his feet gently, his mouth foamed a little. "Keep quiet!" I said in a fury. I might just as well have ordered a tree not to sway in the wind. I darted out. Below me there was a great scuffle of feet on the iron deck; confused exclamations; a voice screamed, "Can you turn back?" I caught sight of a V-shaped ripple on the water ahead. What? Another snag! A fusillade burst out under my feet. The pilgrims had opened with their Winchesters, and were simply squirting lead into that bush. A deuce of a lot of smoke came up and drove slowly forward. I swore at it. Now I couldn't see the ripple or the snag either. I stood in the doorway, peering, and the arrows came in swarms. They might have been poisoned, but they looked as though they wouldn't kill a cat. The bush began to howl. Our wood-cutters raised a warlike whoop; the report of a rifle just at my back deafened me. I glanced over my shoulder, and the pilot-house was yet full of noise and smoke when I made a dash at the wheel. The fool negro had dropped everything, to throw the shutter open and let off that Martini-Henry. He stood before the wide opening, glaring, and I yelled at him to come back, while I straightened the sudden twist out of that steamboat. There was no room to turn even if I had wanted to, the snag was somewhere very near ahead in that confounded smoke, there was no time to lose, so I just crowded her into the bank—right into the bank, where I knew the water was deep.

'We tore slowly along the overhanging bushes in a whirl of broken twigs and flying leaves. The fusillade below stopped short, as I had foreseen it would when the squirts got empty. I threw my head back to a glinting whizz that traversed the pilot-house, in at one shutter-hole and out at the other. Looking past that mad helmsman, who was shaking the empty rifle and yelling at the shore, I saw vague forms of men running bent double, leaping, gliding, distinct, incomplete, evanescent.

PILGRIM

Something big appeared in the air before the shutter, the rifle went overboard, and the man stepped back swiftly, looked at me over his shoulder in an extraordinary, profound, familiar manner, and fell upon my feet. The side of his head hit the wheel twice, and the end of what appeared a long cane clattered round and knocked over a little camp-stool. It looked as though after wrenching that thing from somebody ashore he had lost his balance in the effort. The thin smoke had blown away, we were clear of the snag, and looking ahead I could see that in another hundred yards or so I would be free to sheer off, away from the bank; but my feet felt so very warm and wet that I had to look down. The man had rolled on his back and stared straight up at me; both his hands clutched that cane. It was the shaft of a spear that, either thrown or lunged through the opening, had caught him in the side just below the ribs; the blade had gone in out of sight, after making a frightful gash; my shoes were full; a pool of blood lay very still, gleaming dark-red under the wheel; his eyes shone with an amazing lustre. The fusillade burst out again. He looked at me anxiously, gripping the spear like something precious, with an air of being afraid I would try to take it away from him. I had to make an effort to free my eyes from his gaze and attend to the steering. With one hand I felt above my head for the line of the steam whistle, and jerked out screech after screech hurriedly. The tumult of angry and warlike yells was checked instantly, and then from the depths of the woods went out such a tremulous and prolonged wail of mournful fear and utter despair as may be imagined to follow the flight of the last hope from the earth. There was a great commotion in the bush; the shower of arrows stopped, a few dropping shots rang out sharply—then silence, in which the languid beat of the stern-wheel came plainly to my ears. I put the helm hard a-starboard at the moment

D

when the pilgrim in pink pyjamas, very hot and agitated, appeared in the doorway. "The manager sends me——" he began in an official tone, and stopped short. "Good God!" he said, glaring at the wounded man.

'We two whites stood over him, and his lustrous and inquiring glance enveloped us both. I declare it looked as though he would presently put to us some question in an understandable language; but he died without uttering a sound, without moving a limb, without twitching a muscle. Only in the very last moment, as though in response to some sign we could not see, to some whisper we could not hear, he frowned heavily, and that frown gave to his black death-mask an inconceivably sombre, brooding, and menacing expression. The lustre of inquiring glance faded swiftly into vacant glassiness. "Can you steer?" I asked the agent eagerly. He looked very dubious; but I made a grab at his arm, and he understood at once I meant him to steer whether or no. To tell you the truth, I was morbidly anxious to change my shoes and socks. "He is dead," murmured the fellow, immensely impressed. "No doubt about it," said I, tugging like mad at the shoe-laces. "And by the way, I suppose Mr Kurtz is dead as well by this time."

'For the moment that was the dominant thought. There was a sense of extreme disappointment, as though I had found out I had been striving after something altogether without a substance. I couldn't have been more disgusted if I had travelled all this way for the sole purpose of talking with Mr Kurtz. Talking with . . . I flung one shoe overboard, and became aware that that was exactly what I had been looking forward to—a talk with Kurtz. I made the strange discovery that I had never imagined him as doing, you know, but as discoursing. I didn't say to myself, "Now I will never see him", or "Now I will never shake him by the hand", but, "Now I will never

hear him". The man presented himself as a voice. Not of
course that I did not connect him with some sort of action.
Hadn't I been told in all the tones of jealousy and admiration that he had collected, bartered, swindled, or stolen
more ivory than all the other agents together? That was
not the point. The point was in his being a gifted creature,
and that of all his gifts the one that stood out pre-
eminently, that carried with it a sense of real presence, was
his ability to talk, his words—the gift of expression, the
bewildering, the illuminating, the most exalted and the
most contemptible, the pulsating stream of light, or the
deceitful flow from the heart of an impenetrable darkness.

'The other shoe went flying unto the devil-god of that
river. I thought, "By Jove! it's all over. We are too late;
he has vanished—the gift has vanished, by means of some
spear, arrow, or club. I will never hear that chap speak
after all"—and my sorrow had a startling extravagance
of emotion, even such as I had noticed in the howling
sorrow of these savages in the bush. I couldn't have felt
more of lonely desolation somehow, had I been robbed of
a belief or had missed my destiny in life. . . . Why do you
sigh in this beastly way, somebody? Absurd? Well,
absurd. Good Lord! mustn't a man ever—— Here, give
me some tobacco.' . . .

There was a pause of profound stillness, then a match
flared, and Marlow's lean face appeared, worn, hollow,
with downward folds and dropped eyelids, with an aspect
of concentrated attention; and as he took vigorous draws
at his pipe, it seemed to retreat and advance out of the
night in the regular flicker of the tiny flame. The match
went out.

'Absurd!' he cried. 'This is the worst of trying to tell. . . .
Here you all are, each moored with two good addresses,
like a hulk with two anchors, a butcher round one corner,
a policeman round another, excellent appetites, and

temperature normal—you hear—normal from year's
end to year's end. And you say, Absurd! Absurd be—
exploded! Absurd! My dear boys, what can you expect
from a man who out of sheer nervousness had just flung
overboard a pair of new shoes! Now I think of it, it is
amazing I did not shed tears. I am, upon the whole,
proud of my fortitude. I was cut to the quick at the idea
of having lost the inestimable privilege of listening to the
gifted Kurtz. Of course I was wrong. The privilege was
waiting for me. Oh yes, I heard more than enough. And
I was right, too. A voice. He was very little more than a
voice. And I heard—him—it—this voice—other voices—
all of them were so little more than voices—and the
memory of that time itself lingers around me, impalpable,
like a dying vibration of one immense jabber, silly, atrocious, sordid, savage, or simply mean, without any kind of
sense. Voices, voices—even the girl herself—now——'

He was silent for a long time.

'I laid the ghost of his gifts at last with a lie,' he began
suddenly. 'Girl! What? Did I mention a girl? Oh, she
is out of it—completely. They—the women, I mean—
are out of it—should be out of it. We must help them to
stay in that beautiful world of their own, lest ours gets
worse. Oh, she had to be out of it. You should have heard
the disinterred body of Mr Kurtz saying, "My Intended".
You would have perceived directly then how completely
she was out of it. And the lofty frontal bone of Mr Kurtz!
They say the hair goes on growing sometimes, but this—
ah—specimen, was impressively bald. The wilderness
had patted him on the head, and, behold, it was like a
ball—an ivory ball; it had caressed him, and—lo!—he
had withered; it had taken him, loved him, embraced
him, got into his veins, consumed his flesh, and sealed his
soul to its own by the inconceivable ceremonies of some
devilish initiation. He was its spoiled and pampered

favourite. Ivory? I should think so. Heaps of it, stacks of
it. The old mud shanty was bursting with it. You would
think there was not a single tusk left either above or below
the ground in the whole country. "Mostly fossil," the
manager had remarked, disparagingly. It was no more
fossil than I am; but they call it fossil when it is dug up.
It appears these negroes do bury the tusks sometimes—
but evidently they couldn't bury this parcel deep enough
to save the gifted Mr Kurtz from his fate. We filled the
steamboat with it, and had to pile a lot on the deck. Thus
he could see and enjoy as long as he could see, because the
appreciation of this favour had remained with him to the
last. You should have heard him say, "My ivory". Oh
yes, I heard him. "My Intended, my ivory, my station,
my river, my——" everything belonged to him. It made
me hold my breath in expectation of hearing the wilderness burst into a prodigious peal of laughter that would
shake the fixed stars in their places. Everything belonged
to him—but that was a trifle. The thing was to know what
he belonged to, how many powers of darkness claimed
him for their own. That was the reflection that made you
creepy all over. It was impossible—it was not good for
one either—trying to imagine. He had taken a high seat
amongst the devils of the land—I mean literally. You
can't understand. How could you?—with solid pavement
under your feet, surrounded by kind neighbours ready to
cheer you or to fall on you, stepping delicately between
the butcher and the policeman, in the holy terror of
scandal and gallows and lunatic asylums—how can you
imagine what particular region of the first ages a man's
untrammelled feet may take him into by the way of
solitude—utter solitude without a policeman—by the
way of silence—utter silence, where no warning voice of
a kind neighbour can be heard whispering of public
opinion? These little things make all the great difference.

When they are gone you must fall back upon your own innate strength, upon your own capacity for faithfulness. Of course you may be too much of a fool to go wrong— too dull even to know you are being assaulted by the powers of darkness. I take it, no fool ever made a bargain for his soul with the devil: the fool is too much of a fool, or the devil too much of a devil—I don't know which. Or you may be such a thunderingly exalted creature as to be altogether deaf and blind to anything but heavenly sights and sounds. Then the earth for you is only a standing place—and whether to be like this is your loss or your gain I won't pretend to say. But most of us are neither one nor the other. The earth for us is a place to live in, where we must put up with sights, with sounds, with smells, too, by Jove!—breathe dead hippo, so to speak, and not be contaminated. And there, don't you see, your strength comes in, the faith in your ability for the digging of un-ostentatious holes to bury the stuff in—your power of devotion, not to yourself, but to an obscure, back-breaking business. And that's difficult enough. Mind, I am not trying to excuse or even explain—I am trying to account to myself for—for—Mr Kurtz—for the shade of Mr Kurtz. This initiated wraith from the back of Nowhere honoured me with its amazing confidence before it vanished alto-gether. This was because it could speak English to me. The original Kurtz had been educated partly in England, and —as he was good enough to say himself—his sympathies were in the right place. His mother was half English, his father was half French. All Europe contributed to the making of Kurtz; and by and by I learned that, most appropriately, the International Society for the Suppres-sion of Savage Customs had entrusted him with the making of a report, for its future guidance. And he had written it, too. I've seen it. I've read it. It was eloquent, vibrating with eloquence, but too high-strung, I think. Seventeen

pages of close writing he had found time for! But this
must have been before his—let us say—nerves, went
wrong, and caused him to preside at certain midnight
dances ending with unspeakable rites, which—as far as
I reluctantly gathered from what I heard at various times
—were offered up to him—do you understand?—to Mr
Kurtz himself. But it was a beautiful piece of writing. The
opening paragraph, however, in the light of later information, strikes me now as ominous. He began with the argument that we whites, from the point of development we
had arrived at, "must necessarily appear to them [savages]
in the nature of supernatural beings—we approach them
with the might as of a deity", and so on, and so on. "By
the simple exercise of our will we can exert a power for
good practically unbounded," etc. etc. From that point
he soared and took me with him. The peroration was
magnificent, though difficult to remember, you know. It
gave me the notion of an exotic Immensity ruled by an
august Benevolence. It made me tingle with enthusiasm.
This was the unbounded power of eloquence—of words—
of burning noble words. There were no practical hints to
interrupt the magic current of phrases, unless a kind of
note at the foot of the last page, scrawled evidently much
later, in an unsteady hand, may be regarded as the
exposition of a method. It was very simple, and at the
end of that moving appeal to every altruistic sentiment it
blazed at you, luminous and terrifying, like a flash of
lightning in a serene sky: "Exterminate all the brutes!"
The curious part was that he had apparently forgotten
all about that valuable postscriptum, because, later on,
when he in a sense came to himself, he repeatedly entreated me to take good care of "my pamphlet" (he
called it), as it was sure to have in the future a good
influence upon his career. I had full information about
all these things, and, besides, as it turned out, I was to

have the care of his memory. I've done enough for it to give me the indisputable right to lay it, if I choose, for an everlasting rest in the dustbin of progress, amongst all the sweepings and, figuratively speaking, all the dead cats of civilization. But then, you see, I can't choose. He won't be forgotten. Whatever he was, he was not common. He had the power to charm or frighten rudimentary souls into an aggravated witch-dance in his honour; he could also fill the small souls of the pilgrims with bitter misgivings: he had one devoted friend at least, and he had conquered one soul in the world that was neither rudimentary nor tainted with self-seeking. No; I can't forget him, though I am not prepared to affirm the fellow was exactly worth the life we lost in getting to him. I missed my late helmsman awfully—I missed him even while his body was still lying in the pilot-house. Perhaps you will think it passing strange, this regret for a savage who was no more account than a grain of sand in a black Sahara. Well, don't you see, he had done something, he had steered; for months I had him at my back—a help—an instrument. It was a kind of partnership. He steered for me—I had to look after him, I worried about his deficiencies, and thus a subtle bond had been created, of which I only became aware when it was suddenly broken. And the intimate profundity of that look he gave me when he received his hurt remains to this day in my memory —like a claim of distant kinship affirmed in a supreme moment.

'Poor fool! If he had only left that shutter alone. He had no restraint, no restraint—just like Kurtz—a tree swayed by the wind. As soon as I had put on a dry pair of slippers I dragged him out, after first jerking the spear out of his side, which operation I confess I performed with my eyes shut tight. His heels leaped together over the little door-step; his shoulders were pressed to my breast; I hugged him from behind desperately. Oh, he was heavy, heavy; heavier than any man on earth, I should imagine. Then without more ado I tipped him overboard. The current snatched him as though he had been a wisp of grass, and I saw the body roll over twice before I lost sight of it for ever. All the pilgrims and the manager were then congregated on the awning-deck about the pilot-house, chattering at each other like a flock of excited magpies, and there was a scandalized murmur at my heartless promptitude. What they wanted to keep that body hanging about for I can't guess. Embalm it, maybe. But I had also heard another, and a very ominous, murmur on the deck below. My friends the wood-cutters were likewise scandalized, and with a better show of reason—though I admit that the reason itself was quite inadmissible. Oh, quite! I had made up my mind that if my late helmsman was to be eaten, the fishes alone should have him. He had been a very second-rate helmsman while alive, but now he was dead he might have become a first-class temptation, and possibly cause some startling trouble. Besides, I was anxious to take the wheel, the man in pink pyjamas showing himself a hopeless duffer at the business.

'This I did directly the simple funeral was over. We were going half-speed, keeping right in the middle of the stream, and I listened to the talk about me. They had given up Kurtz, they had given up the station; Kurtz was dead, and the station had been burnt—and so on—and so on. The red-haired pilgrim was beside himself with the thought that at least this poor Kurtz had been properly avenged. "Say! We must have made a glorious slaughter of them in the bush. Eh? What do you think? Say?" He positively danced, the bloodthirsty little gingery beggar. And he had nearly fainted when he saw the wounded man! I could not help saying, "You made a

* D

glorious lot of smoke, anyhow." I had seen, from the way the tops of the bushes rustled and flew, that almost all the shots had gone too high. You can't hit anything unless you take aim and fire from the shoulder; but these chaps fired from the hip with their eyes shut. The retreat, I maintained—and I was right—was caused by the screeching of the steam whistle. Upon this they forgot Kurtz, and began to howl at me with indignant protests.

'The manager stood by the wheel murmuring confidentially about the necessity of getting well away down the river before dark at all events, when I saw in the distance a clearing on the riverside and the outlines of some sort of building. "What's this?" I asked. He clapped his hands in wonder. "The station!" he cried. I edged in at once, still going half-speed.

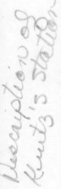

'Through my glasses I saw the slope of a hill interspersed with rare trees and perfectly free from undergrowth. A long decaying building on the summit was half buried in the high grass; the large holes in the peaked roof gaped black from afar; the jungle and the woods made a background. There was no enclosure or fence of any kind; but there had been one apparently, for near the house half a dozen slim posts remained in a row, roughly trimmed, and with their upper ends ornamented with round carved balls. The rails, or whatever there had been between, had disappeared. Of course the forest surrounded all that. The river-bank was clear, and on the waterside I saw a white man under a hat like a cart-wheel beckoning persistently with his whole arm. Examining the edge of the forest above and below, I was almost certain I could see movements—human forms gliding here and there. I steamed past prudently, then stopped the engines and let her drift down. The man on the shore began to shout, urging us to land. "We have been attacked!" screamed the manager. "I know—I know. It's all right!" yelled back the other,

as cheerful as you please. "Come along. It's all right.
I am glad."

'His aspect reminded me of something I had seen—
something funny I had seen somewhere. As I manœuvred
to get alongside, I was asking myself, "What does this
fellow look like?" Suddenly I got it. He looked like a
harlequin. His clothes had been made of some stuff that
was brown holland probably, but it was covered with
patches all over, with bright patches, blue, red, and yellow
—patches on the back, patches on the front, patches on
elbows, on knees; coloured binding around his jacket,
scarlet edging at the bottom of his trousers; and the sunshine made him look extremely gay and wonderfully neat
withal, because you could see how beautifully all this
patching had been done. A beardless, boyish face, very
fair, no features to speak of, nose peeling, little blue eyes,
smiles and frowns chasing each other over that open
countenance like sunshine and shadow on a wind-swept
plain. "Look out, captain!" he cried; "there's a snag
lodged in here last night." What! Another snag? I confess
I swore shamefully. I had nearly holed my cripple, to
finish off that charming trip. The harlequin on the bank
turned his little pug-nose up to me. "You English?" he
asked, all smiles. "Are you?" I shouted from the wheel.
The smiles vanished, and he shook his head as if sorry for
my disappointment. Then he brightened up. "Never
mind!" he cried, encouragingly. "Are we in time?" I
asked. "He is up there," he replied, with a toss of the
head up the hill, and becoming gloomy all of a sudden.
His face was like the autumn sky, overcast one moment
and bright the next.

'When the manager, escorted by the pilgrims, all of
them armed to the teeth, had gone to the house this chap
came on board. "I say, I don't like this. These natives
are in the bush," I said. He assured me earnestly it was

all right. "They are simple people," he added; "well, I am glad you came. It took me all my time to keep them off." "But you said it was all right," I cried. "Oh, they meant no harm," he said; and as I stared he corrected himself: "Not exactly." Then vivaciously: "My faith, your pilot-house wants a clean up!" In the next breath he advised me to keep enough steam on the boiler to blow the whistle in case of any trouble. "One good screech will do more for you than all your rifles. They are simple people," he repeated. He rattled away at such a rate he quite overwhelmed me. He seemed to be trying to make up for lots of silence, and actually hinted, laughing, that such was the case. "Don't you talk with Mr Kurtz?" I said. "You don't talk with that man—you listen to him," he exclaimed with severe exaltation. "But now——" He waved his arm, and in the twinkling of an eye was in the uttermost depths of despondency. In a moment he came up again with a jump, possessed himself of both my hands, shook them continuously, while he gabbled: "Brother sailor . . . honour . . . pleasure . . . delight . . . introduce myself . . . Russian . . . son of an arch-priest . . . Government of Tambov . . . What? Tobacco! English tobacco; the excellent English tobacco! Now, that's brotherly. Smoke? Where's a sailor that does not smoke?"

'The pipe soothed him, and gradually I made out he had run away from school, had gone to sea in a Russian ship; ran away again; served some time in English ships; was now reconciled with the arch-priest. He made a point of that. "But when one is young one must see things, gather experience, ideas; enlarge the mind." "Here!" I interrupted. "You can never tell! Here I met Mr Kurtz," he said, youthfully solemn and reproachful. I held my tongue after that. It appears he had persuaded a Dutch trading-house on the coast to fit him out with stores and goods, and had started for the interior with a light heart, and no more idea of what would happen to him than a baby. He had been wandering about that river for nearly two years alone, cut off from everybody and everything. "I am not so young as I look. I am twenty-five," he said. "At first old Van Shuyten would tell me to go to the devil," he narrated with keen enjoyment; "but I stuck to him, and talked and talked, till at last he got afraid I would talk the hind-leg off his favourite dog, so he gave me some cheap things and a few guns, and told me he hoped he would never see my face again. Good old Dutchman, Van Shuyten. I've sent him one small lot of ivory a year ago, so that he can't call me a little thief when I get back. I hope he got it. And for the rest I don't care. I had some wood stacked for you. That was my old house. Did you see?"

'I gave him Towson's book. He made as though he would kiss me, but restrained himself. "The only book I had left, and I thought I had lost it," he said, looking at it ecstatically. "So many accidents happen to a man going about alone, you know. Canoes get upset sometimes—and sometimes you've got to clear out so quick when the people get angry." He thumbed the pages. "You made notes in Russian?" I asked. He nodded. "I thought they were written in cipher," I said. He laughed, then became serious. "I had lots of trouble to keep these people off," he said. "Did they want to kill you?" I asked. "Oh no!" he cried, and checked himself. "Why did they attack us?" I pursued. He hesitated, then said shamefacedly: "They don't want him to go." "Don't they?" I said, curiously. He nodded a nod full of mystery and wisdom. "I tell you," he cried, "this man has enlarged my mind." He opened his arms wide, staring at me with his little blue eyes that were perfectly round.'

III

'I LOOKED at him, lost in astonishment. There he was before me, in motley, as though he had absconded from a troupe of mimes, enthusiastic, fabulous. His very existence was improbable, inexplicable, and altogether bewildering. He was an insoluble problem. It was inconceivable how he had existed, how he had succeeded in getting so far, how he had managed to remain—why he did not instantly disappear. "I went a little farther," he said, "then still a little farther—till I had gone so far that I don't know how I'll ever get back. Never mind. Plenty time. I can manage. You take Kurtz away quick—quick—I tell you." The glamour of youth enveloped his particoloured rags, his destitution, his loneliness, the essential desolation of his futile wanderings. For months—for years —his life hadn't been worth a day's purchase; and there he was gallantly, thoughtlessly alive, to all appearance indestructible solely by the virtue of his few years and of his unreflecting audacity. I was seduced into something like admiration—like envy. Glamour urged him on, glamour kept him unscathed. He surely wanted nothing from the wilderness but space to breathe in and to push on through. His need was to exist, and to move onwards at the greatest possible risk, and with a maximum of privation. If the absolutely pure, uncalculating, unpractical spirit of adventure had ever ruled a human being, it ruled this be-patched youth. I almost envied him the possession of this modest and clear flame. It seemed to have consumed all thought of self so completely, that even while he was talking to you, you forgot that it was he— the man before your eyes—who had gone through these things. I did not envy him his devotion to Kurtz, though. He had not meditated over it. It came to him, and he accepted it with a sort of eager fatalism. I must say that to me it appeared about the most dangerous thing in every way he had come upon so far.

'They had come together unavoidably, like two ships becalmed near each other, and lay rubbing sides at last. I suppose Kurtz wanted an audience, because on a certain occasion, when encamped in the forest, they had talked all night, or more probably Kurtz had talked. "We talked of everything," he said, quite transported at the recollection. "I forgot there was such a thing as sleep. The night did not seem to last an hour. Everything! Everything! . . . Of love, too." "Ah, he talked to you of love!" I said, much amused. "It isn't what you think," he cried, almost passionately. "It was in general. He made me see things— things."

'He threw his arms up. We were on deck at the time, and the headman of my wood-cutters, lounging near by, turned upon him his heavy and glittering eyes. I looked around, and I don't know why, but I assure you that never, never before, did this land, this river, this jungle, the very arch of this blazing sky, appear to me so hopeless and so dark, so impenetrable to human thought, so pitiless to human weakness. "And, ever since, you have been with him, of course?" I said.

'On the contrary. It appears their intercourse had been very much broken by various causes. He had, as he informed me proudly, managed to nurse Kurtz through two illnesses (he alluded to it as you would to some risky feat), but as a rule Kurtz wandered alone, far in the depths of the forest. "Very often coming to this station, I had to wait days and days before he would turn up," he said. "Ah, it was worth waiting for!—sometimes." "What was he doing? Exploring or what?" I asked. "Oh yes, of course"; he had discovered lots of villages, a lake, too— he did not know exactly in what direction; it was danger- ous to inquire too much—but mostly his expeditions had been for ivory. "But he had no goods to trade with by that time," I objected. "There's a good lot of cartridges left even yet," he answered, looking away. "To speak plainly, he raided the country," I said. He nodded. "Not alone, surely!" He muttered something about the villages round that lake. "Kurtz got the tribe to follow him, did he?" I suggested. He fidgeted a little. "They adored him," he said. The tone of these words was so extraordinary that I looked at him searchingly. It was curious to see his mingled eagerness and reluctance to speak of Kurtz. The man filled his life, occupied his thoughts, swayed his emotions. "What can you expect?" he burst out. "He came to them with thunder and lightning, you know— and they had never seen anything like it—and very terrible. He could be very terrible. You can't judge Mr Kurtz as you would an ordinary man. No, no, no! Now— just to give you an idea—I don't mind telling you, he wanted to shoot me, too, one day—but I don't judge him." "Shoot you!" I cried. "What for?" "Well, I had a small lot of ivory the chief of that village near my house gave me. You see I used to shoot game for them. Well, he wanted it, and wouldn't hear reason. He declared he would shoot me unless I gave him the ivory and then cleared out of the country, because he could do so, and had a fancy for it, and there was nothing on earth to prevent him killing whom he jolly well pleased. And it was true, too. I gave him the ivory. What did I care!

But I didn't clear out. No, no. I couldn't leave him. I had
to be careful, of course, till we got friendly again for a
time. He had his second illness then. Afterwards I had to
keep out of the way; but I didn't mind. He was living for
the most part in those villages on the lake. When he came
down to the river, sometimes he would take to me, and
sometimes it was better for me to be careful. This man
suffered too much. He hated all this, and somehow he
couldn't get away. When I had a chance I begged him to
try and leave while there was time; I offered to go back
with him. And he would say yes, and then he would
remain; go off on another ivory hunt; disappear for
weeks; forget himself amongst these people—forget himself—you know." "Why, he's mad," I said. He protested
indignantly. Mr Kurtz couldn't be mad. If I had heard
him talk, only two days ago, I wouldn't dare hint at such
a thing. . . . I had taken up my binoculars while we talked,
and was looking at the shore, sweeping the limit of the
forest at each side and at the back of the house. The con-
sciousness of there being people in that bush, so silent, so
quiet—as silent and quiet as the ruined house on the hill
—made me uneasy. There was no sign on the face of
nature of this amazing tale that was not so much told as
suggested to me in desolate exclamations, completed by
shrugs, in interrupted phrases, in hints ending in deep
sighs. The woods were unmoved, like a mask—heavy,
like the closed door of a prison—they looked with their
air of hidden knowledge, of patient expectation, of un-
approachable silence. The Russian was explaining to me
that it was only lately that Mr Kurtz had come down to the
river, bringing along with him all the fighting men of that
lake tribe. He had been absent for several months—getting
himself adored, I suppose—and had come down unexpectedly, with the intention to all appearance of making a
raid either across the river or downstream. Evidently the

appetite for more ivory had got the better of the—what shall I say?—less material aspirations. However, he had got much worse suddenly. "I heard he was lying helpless, and so I came up—took my chance," said the Russian. "Oh, he is bad, very bad." I directed my glass to the house. There were no signs of life, but there was the ruined roof, the long mud wall peeping above the grass, with three little square window holes, no two of the same size; all this brought within reach of my hand, as it were. And then I made a brusque movement, and one of the remaining posts of that vanished fence leaped up in the field of my glass. You remember I told you I had been struck at the distance by certain attempts at ornamentation, rather remarkable in the ruinous aspect of the place. Now I had suddenly a nearer view, and its first result was to make me throw my head back as if before a blow. Then I went carefully from post to post with my glass, and I saw my mistake. These round knobs were not ornamental but symbolic; they were expressive and puzzling, striking and disturbing—food for thought and also for the vultures if there had been any looking down from the sky; but at all events for such ants as were industrious enough to ascend the pole. They would have been even more impressive, those heads on the stakes, if their faces had not been turned to the house. Only one, the first I had made out, was facing my way. I was not so shocked as you may think. The start back I had given was really nothing but a movement of surprise. I had expected to see a knob of wood there, you know. I returned deliberately to the first I had seen—and there it was, black, dried, sunken, with closed eyelids—a head that seemed to sleep at the top of that pole, and, with the shrunken dry lips showing a narrow white line of the teeth, was smiling, too, smiling continuously at some endless and jocose dream of that eternal slumber.

'I am not disclosing any trade secrets. In fact, the

manager said afterwards that Mr Kurtz's methods had ruined the district. I have no opinion on that point, but I want you clearly to understand that there was nothing exactly profitable in these heads being there. They only showed that Mr Kurtz lacked restraint in the gratification of his various lusts, that there was something wanting in him—some small matter which, when the pressing need arose, could not be found under his magnificent eloquence. Whether he knew of this deficiency himself I can't say. I think the knowledge came to him at last—only at the very last. But the wilderness had found him out early, and had taken on him a terrible vengeance for the fantastic invasion. I think it had whispered to him things about himself which he did not know, things of which he had no conception till he took counsel with this great solitude—and the whisper had proved irresistibly fascinating. It echoed loudly within him because he was hollow at the core. . . . I put down the glass, and the head that had appeared near enough to be spoken to seemed at once to have leaped away from me into inaccessible distance.

'The admirer of Mr Kurtz was a bit crestfallen. In a hurried, indistinct voice he began to assure me he had not dared to take these—say, symbols—down. He was not afraid of the natives; they would not stir till Mr Kurtz gave the word. His ascendancy was extraordinary. The camps of these people surrounded the place, and the chiefs came every day to see him. They would crawl. . . . "I don't want to know anything of the ceremonies used when approaching Mr Kurtz!" I shouted. Curious, this feeling that came over me that such details would be more intolerable than those heads drying on the stakes under Mr Kurtz's windows. After all, that was only a savage sight, while I seemed at one bound to have been transported into some lightless region of subtle horrors, where pure, uncomplicated savagery was a positive relief, being something that had a right to exist—obviously—in the sunshine. The young man looked at me with surprise. I suppose it did not occur to him that Mr Kurtz was no idol of mine. He forgot I hadn't heard any of these splendid monologues on—what was it?—on love, justice, conduct of life—or what not. If it had come to crawling before Mr Kurtz, he crawled as much as the veriest savage of them all. I had no idea of the conditions, he said: these heads were the heads of rebels. I shocked him excessively by laughing. Rebels! What would be the next definition I was to hear? There had been enemies, criminals, workers —and these were rebels. Those rebellious heads looked very subdued to me on their sticks. "You don't know how such a life tries a man like Kurtz," cried Kurtz's last disciple. "Well, and you?" I said. "I! I! I am a simple man. I have no great thoughts. I want nothing from anybody. How can you compare me to——" His feelings were too much for speech, and suddenly he broke down. "I don't understand," he groaned. "I've been doing my best to keep him alive, and that's enough. I had no hand in all this. I have no abilities. There hasn't been a drop of medicine or a mouthful of invalid food for months here. He was shamefully abandoned. A man like this, with such ideas. Shamefully! Shamefully! I—I—haven't slept for the last ten nights. . . ."

'His voice lost itself in the calm of the evening. The long shadows of the forest had slipped downhill while we talked, had gone far beyond the ruined hovel, beyond the symbolic row of stakes. All this was in the gloom, while we down there were yet in the sunshine, and the stretch of the river abreast of the clearing glittered in a still and dazzling splendour, with a murky and overshadowed bend above and below. Not a living soul was seen on the shore. The bushes did not rustle.

'Suddenly round the corner of the house a group of

men appeared, as though they had come up from the ground. They waded waist deep in the grass, in a compact body, bearing an improvised stretcher in their midst. Instantly, in the emptiness of the landscape, a cry arose whose shrillness pierced the still air like a sharp arrow flying straight to the very heart of the land; and, as if by enchantment, streams of human beings—of naked human beings—with spears in their hands, with bows, with shields, with wild glances and savage movements, were poured into the clearing by the dark-faced and pensive forest. The bushes shook, the grass swayed for a time, and then everything stood still in attentive immobility.

'"Now, if he does not say the right thing to them we are all done for," said the Russian at my elbow. The knot of men with the stretcher had stopped, too, half way to the steamer, as if petrified. I saw the man on the stretcher sit up, lank and with an uplifted arm, above the shoulders of the bearers. "Let us hope that the man who can talk so well of love in general will find some particular reason to spare us this time," I said. I resented bitterly the absurd danger of our situation as if to be at the mercy of that atrocious phantom had been a dishonouring necessity. I could not hear a sound, but through my glasses I saw the thin arm extended commandingly, the lower jaw moving, the eyes of that apparition shining darkly far in its bony head that nodded with grotesque jerks. Kurtz—Kurtz— that means short in German—don't it? Well, the name was as true as everything else in his life—and death. He looked at least seven feet long. His covering had fallen off, and his body emerged from it pitiful and appalling as from a winding-sheet. I could see the cage of his ribs all astir, the bones of his arm waving. It was as though an animated image of death carved out of old ivory had been shaking its hand with menaces at a motionless crowd of men made of dark and glittering bronze. I saw him open his mouth wide—it gave him a weirdly voracious aspect, as though he had wanted to swallow all the air, all the earth, all the men before him. A deep voice reached me faintly. He must have been shouting. He fell back suddenly. The stretcher shook as the bearers staggered forward again, and almost at the same time I noticed that the crowd of savages was vanishing without any perceptible movement of retreat, as if the forest that had ejected these beings so suddenly had drawn them in again as the breath is drawn in a long aspiration.

'Some of the pilgrims behind the stretcher carried his arms—two shot-guns, a heavy rifle, and a light revolver-carbine—the thunderbolts of that pitiful Jupiter. The manager bent over him murmuring as he walked beside his head. They laid him down in one of the little cabins—just a room for a bedplace and a camp-stool or two, you know. We had brought his belated correspondence, and a lot of torn envelopes and open letters littered his bed. His hand roamed feebly amongst these papers. I was struck by the fire of his eyes and the composed languor of his expression. It was not so much the exhaustion of disease. He did not seem in pain. This shadow looked satiated and calm, as though for the moment it had had its fill of all the emotions.

'He rustled one of the letters, and looking straight in my face said: "I am glad." Somebody had been writing to him about me. These special recommendations were turning up again. The volume of tone he emitted without effort, almost without the trouble of moving his lips, amazed me. A voice! a voice! It was grave, profound, vibrating, while the man did not seem capable of a whisper. However, he had enough strength in him—factitious no doubt—to very nearly make an end of us, as you shall hear directly.

'The manager appeared silently in the doorway; I

stepped out at once and he drew the curtain after me. The Russian, eyed curiously by the pilgrims, was staring at the shore. I followed the direction of his glance.

'Dark human shapes could be made out in the distance, flitting indistinctly against the gloomy border of the forest, and near the river two bronze figures, leaning on tall spears, stood in the sunlight under fantastic head-dresses of spotted skins, warlike and still in statuesque repose. And from right to left along the lighted shore moved a wild and gorgeous apparition of a woman.

'She walked with measured steps, draped in striped and fringed cloths, treading the earth proudly, with a slight jingle and flash of barbarous ornaments. She carried her head high; her hair was done in the shape of a helmet; she had brass leggings to the knee, brass wire gauntlets to the elbow, a crimson spot on her tawny cheek, innumerable necklaces of glass beads on her neck; bizarre things, charms, gifts of witch-men, that hung about her, glittered and trembled at every step. She must have had the value of several elephant tusks upon her. She was savage and superb, wild-eyed and magnificent; there was something ominous and stately in her deliberate progress. And in the hush that had fallen suddenly upon the whole sorrowful land, the immense wilderness, the colossal body of the fecund and mysterious life seemed to look at her, pensive, as though it had been looking at the image of its own tenebrous and passionate soul.

'She came abreast of the steamer, stood still, and faced us. Her long shadow fell to the water's edge. Her face had a tragic and fierce aspect of wild sorrow and of dumb pain mingled with the fear of some struggling, half-shaped resolve. She stood looking at us without a stir, and like the wilderness itself, with an air of brooding over an inscrutable purpose. A whole minute passed, and then she made a step forward. There was a low jingle, a glint of yellow metal, a sway of fringed draperies, and she stopped as if her heart had failed her. The young fellow by my side growled. The pilgrims murmured at my back. She looked at us all as if her life had depended upon the unswerving steadiness of her glance. Suddenly she opened her bared arms and threw them up rigid above her head, as though in an uncontrollable desire to touch the sky, and at the same time the swift shadows darted out on the earth, swept around on the river, gathering the steamer into a shadowy embrace. A formidable silence hung over the scene.

'She turned away slowly, walked on, following the bank, and passed into the bushes to the left. Once only her eyes gleamed back at us in the dusk of the thickets before she disappeared.

'"If she had offered to come aboard I really think I would have tried to shoot her," said the man of patches, nervously. "I had been risking my life every day for the last fortnight to keep her out of the house. She got in one day and kicked up a row about those miserable rags I picked up in the storeroom to mend my clothes with. I wasn't decent. At least it must have been that, for she talked like a fury to Kurtz for an hour, pointing at me now and then. I don't understand the dialect of this tribe. Luckily for me, I fancy Kurtz felt too ill that day to care, or there would have been mischief. I don't understand. . . . No—it's too much for me. Ah, well, it's all over now."

'At this moment I heard Kurtz's deep voice behind the curtain: "Save me!—save the ivory, you mean. Don't tell me. Save *me*! Why, I've had to save you. You are interrupting my plans now. Sick! Sick! Not so sick as you would like to believe. Never mind. I'll carry my ideas out yet—I will return. I'll show you what can be done. You with your little peddling notions—you are interfering with me. I will return. I . . ."

'The manager came out. He did me the honour to take me under the arm and lead me aside. "He is very low, very low," he said. He considered it necessary to sigh, but neglected to be consistently sorrowful. "We have done all we could for him—haven't we? But there is no disguising the fact, Mr Kurtz has done more harm than good to the Company. He did not see the time was not ripe for vigorous action. Cautiously, cautiously—that's my principle. We must be cautious yet. The district is closed to us for a time. Deplorable! Upon the whole, the trade will suffer. I don't deny there is a remarkable quantity of ivory—mostly fossil. We must save it, at all events—but look how precarious the position is—and why? Because the method is unsound." "Do you", said I, looking at the shore, "call it 'unsound method?'" "Without doubt!" he exclaimed, hotly. "Don't you?" . . . "No method at all," I murmured after a while. "Exactly," he exulted. "I anticipated this. Shows a complete want of judgment. It is my duty to point it out in the proper quarter." "Oh," said I, "that fellow—what's his name?—the brickmaker, will make a readable report for you." He appeared confounded for a moment. It seemed to me I had never breathed an atmosphere so vile, and I turned mentally to Kurtz for relief—positively for relief. "Nevertheless I think Mr Kurtz is a remarkable man," I said with emphasis. He started, dropped on me a cold heavy glance, said very quietly, "He *was*", and turned his back on me. My hour of favour was over; I found myself lumped along with Kurtz as a partisan of methods for which the time was not ripe: I was unsound! Ah, but it was something to have at least a choice of nightmares.

'I had turned to the wilderness really, not to Mr Kurtz, who, I was ready to admit, was as good as buried. And for a moment it seemed to me as if I also were buried in a vast grave full of unspeakable secrets. I felt an intolerable weight oppressing my breast, the smell of the damp earth, the unseen presence of victorious corruption, the darkness of an impenetrable night. . . . The Russian tapped me on the shoulder. I heard him mumbling and stammering something about "brother seaman—couldn't conceal—knowledge of matters that would affect Mr Kurtz's reputation". I waited. For him evidently Mr Kurtz was not in his grave; I suspect that for him Mr Kurtz was one of the immortals. "Well," said I at last, "speak out. As it happens, I am Mr Kurtz's friend—in a way."

'He stated with a good deal of formality that had we not been "of the same profession", he would have kept the matter to himself without regard to consequences. "He suspected there was an active ill will towards him on the part of these white men that——" "You are right," I said, remembering a certain conversation I had overheard. "The manager thinks you ought to be hanged." He showed a concern at this intelligence which amused me at first. "I had better get out of the way quietly," he said, earnestly. "I can do no more for Kurtz now, and they would soon find some excuse. What's to stop them? There's a military post three hundred miles from here." "Well, upon my word," said I, "perhaps you had better go if you have any friends amongst the savages near by." "Plenty," he said. "They are simple people—and I want nothing, you know." He stood biting his lip, then: "I don't want any harm to happen to these whites here, but of course I was thinking of Mr Kurtz's reputation—but you are a brother seaman and——" "All right," said I, after a time. "Mr Kurtz's reputation is safe with me." I did not know how truly I spoke.

'He informed me, lowering his voice, that it was Kurtz who had ordered the attack to be made on the steamer. "He hated sometimes the idea of being taken away—and then again . . . but I don't understand these matters. I am a simple man. He thought it would scare you away— that you would give it up, thinking him dead. I could not stop him. Oh, I had an awful time of it this last month." "Very well," I said. "He is all right now." "Ye-e-es," he muttered, not very convinced apparently. "Thanks," said I; "I shall keep my eyes open." "But quiet—eh?" he urged, anxiously. "It would be awful for his reputation if anybody here——" I promised a complete discretion with great gravity. "I have a canoe and three black fellows waiting not very far. I am off. Could you give me a few Martini-Henry cartridges?" I could, and did, with proper secrecy. He helped himself, with a wink at me, to a handful of my tobacco. "Between sailors—you know— good English tobacco." At the door of the pilot-house he turned round: "I say, haven't you a pair of shoes you could spare?" He raised one leg. "Look." The soles were tied with knotted strings sandal-wise under his bare feet. I rooted out an old pair, at which he looked with admiration before tucking it under his left arm. One of his pockets (bright red) was bulging with cartridges, from the other (dark blue) peeped "Towson's Inquiry", etc. etc. He seemed to think himself excellently well equipped for a renewed encounter with the wilderness. "Ah, I'll never, never meet such a man again. You ought to have heard him recite poetry—his own, too, it was, he told me. Poetry!" He rolled his eyes at the recollection of these delights. "Oh, he enlarged my mind!" "Goodbye," said I. He shook hands and vanished in the night. Sometimes I ask myself whether I had ever really seen him—whether it was possible to meet such a phenomenon! . . .

'When I woke up shortly after midnight his warning came to my mind with its hint of danger that seemed, in the starred darkness, real enough to make me get up for

the purpose of having a look round. On the hill a big
fire burned, illuminating fitfully a crooked corner of the
station-house. One of the agents with a picket of a few of
our blacks, armed for the purpose, was keeping guard
over the ivory; but deep within the forest, red gleams
that wavered, that seemed to sink and rise from the
ground amongst confused columnar shapes of intense
blackness, showed the exact position of the camp where
Mr Kurtz's adorers were keeping their uneasy vigil. The
monotonous beating of a big drum filled the air with
muffled shocks and a lingering vibration. A steady droning
sound of many men chanting each to himself some weird
incantation came out from the black, flat wall of the woods
as the humming of bees comes out of a hive, and had a
strange narcotic effect upon my half-awake senses. I
believe I dozed off leaning over the rail, till an abrupt
burst of yells, an overwhelming outbreak of a pent-up
and mysterious frenzy, woke me up in a bewildered
wonder. It was cut short all at once, and the low droning
went on with an effect of audible and soothing silence. I
glanced casually into the little cabin. A light was burning
within, but Mr Kurtz was not there.

'I think I would have raised an outcry if I had believed
my eyes. But I didn't believe them at first—the thing
seemed so impossible. The fact is I was completely un-
nerved by a sheer blank fright, pure abstract terror, unconnected with any distinct shape of physical danger.
What made this emotion so overpowering was—how
shall I define it?—the moral shock I received, as if something altogether monstrous, intolerable to thought and
odious to the soul, had been thrust upon me unexpectedly.
This lasted of course the merest fraction of a second, and
then the usual sense of commonplace, deadly danger, the
possibility of a sudden onslaught and massacre, or something of the kind, which I saw impending, was positively

welcome and composing. It pacified me, in fact, so much, that I did not raise an alarm.

'There was an agent buttoned up inside an ulster and sleeping on a chair on deck within three feet of me. The yells had not awakened him; he snored very slightly; I left him to his slumbers and leaped ashore. I did not betray Mr Kurtz—it was ordered I should never betray him—it was written I should be loyal to the nightmare of my choice. I was anxious to deal with this shadow by myself alone—and to this day I don't know why I was so jealous of sharing with anyone the peculiar blackness of that experience.

'As soon as I got on the bank I saw a trail—a broad trail through the grass. I remember the exultation with which I said to myself: "He can't walk—he is crawling on all fours—I've got him." The grass was wet with dew. I strode rapidly with clenched fists. I fancy I had some vague notion of falling upon him and giving him a drubbing. I don't know. I had some imbecile thoughts. The knitting old woman with the cat obtruded herself upon my memory as a most improper person to be sitting at the other end of such an affair. I saw a row of pilgrims squirting lead in the air out of Winchesters held to the hip. I thought I would never get back to the steamer, and imagined myself living alone and unarmed in the woods to an advanced age. Such silly things—you know. And I remember I confounded the beat of the drum with the beating of my heart, and was pleased at its calm regularity.

'I kept to the track though—then stopped to listen. The night was very clear: a dark blue space, sparkling with dew and starlight, in which black things stood very still. I thought I could see a kind of motion ahead of me. I was strangely cocksure of everything that night. I actually left the track and ran in a wide semicircle (I verily believe chuckling to myself) so as to get in front of that stir, of that motion I had seen—if indeed I had seen anything. I was circumventing Kurtz as though it had been a boyish game.

'I came upon him, and, if he had not heard me coming, I would have fallen over him, too, but he got up in time. He rose, unsteady, long, pale, indistinct, like a vapour exhaled by the earth, and swayed slightly, misty and silent before me; while at my back the fires loomed between the trees, and the murmur of many voices issued from the forest. I had cut him off cleverly; but when actually confronting him I seemed to come to my senses, I saw the danger in its right proportion. It was by no means over yet. Suppose he began to shout? Though he could hardly stand, there was still plenty of vigour in his voice. "Go away—hide yourself," he said, in that profound tone. It was very awful. I glanced back. We were within thirty yards from the nearest fire. A black figure stood up, strode on long black legs, waving long black arms, across the glow. It had horns—antelope horns, I think—on its head. Some sorcerer, some witch-man, no doubt: it looked fiend-like enough. "Do you know what you are doing?" I whispered. "Perfectly," he answered, raising his voice for that single word: it sounded to me far off and yet loud, like a hail through a speaking-trumpet. If he makes a row we are lost, I thought to myself. This clearly was not a case for fisticuffs, even apart from the very natural aversion I had to beat that Shadow—this wandering and tormented thing. "You will be lost," I said, "utterly lost." One gets sometimes such a flash of inspiration, you know. I did say the right thing, though indeed he could not have been more irretrievably lost than he was at this very moment, when the foundations of our intimacy were being laid—to endure—to endure—even to the end—even beyond.

'"I had immense plans," he muttered irresolutely.

"Yes," said I; "but if you try to shout I'll smash your head with——" There was not a stick or a stone near. "I will throttle you for good," I corrected myself. "I was on the threshold of great things," he pleaded, in a voice of longing, with a wistfulness of tone that made my blood run cold. "And now for this stupid scoundrel——" "Your success in Europe is assured in any case," I affirmed, steadily. I did not want to have the throttling of him, you understand—and indeed it would have been very little use for any practical purpose. I tried to break the spell—the heavy, mute spell of the wilderness—that seemed to draw him to its pitiless breast by the awakening of forgotten and brutal instincts, by the memory of gratified and monstrous passions. This alone, I was convinced, had driven him out to the edge of the forest, to the bush, towards the gleam of fires, the throb of drums, the drone of weird incantations; this alone had beguiled his unlawful soul beyond the bounds of permitted aspirations. And, don't you see, the terror of the position was not in being knocked on the head—though I had a very lively sense of that danger, too—but in this, that I had to deal with a being to whom I could not appeal in the name of anything high or low. I had, even like the negroes, to invoke him—himself—his own exalted and incredible degradation. There was nothing either above or below him, and I knew it. He had kicked himself loose of the earth. Confound the man! he had kicked the very earth to pieces. He was alone, and I before him did not know whether I stood on the ground or floated in the air. I've been telling you what we said—repeating the phrases we pronounced—but what's the good? They were common everyday words—the familiar, vague sounds exchanged on every waking day of life. But what of that? They had behind them, to my mind, the terrific suggestiveness of words heard in dreams, of phrases spoken in nightmares. Soul!

If anybody had ever struggled with a soul, I am the man. And I wasn't arguing with a lunatic either. Believe me or not, his intelligence was perfectly clear—concentrated, it is true, upon himself with horrible intensity, yet clear; and therein was my only chance—barring, of course, the killing him there and then, which wasn't so good, on account of unavoidable noise. But his soul was mad. Being alone in the wilderness, it had looked within itself, and, by heavens! I tell you, it had gone mad. I had—for my sins, I suppose—to go through the ordeal of looking into it myself. No eloquence could have been so withering to one's belief in mankind as his final burst of sincerity. He struggled with himself, too. I saw it—I heard it. I saw the inconceivable mystery of a soul that knew no restraint, no faith, and no fear, yet struggling blindly with itself. I kept my head pretty well; but when I had him at last stretched on the couch, I wiped my forehead, while my legs shook under me as though I had carried half a ton on my back down that hill. And yet I had only supported him, his bony arm clasped round my neck—and he was not much heavier than a child.

'When next day we left at noon, the crowd, of whose presence behind the curtain of trees I had been acutely conscious all the time, flowed out of the woods again, filled the clearing, covered the slope with a mass of naked, breathing, quivering, bronze bodies. I steamed up a bit, then swung downstream, and two thousand eyes followed the evolutions of the splashing, thumping, fierce river-demon beating the water with its terrible tail and breathing black smoke into the air. In front of the first rank, along the river, three men, plastered with bright red earth from head to foot, strutted to and fro restlessly. When we came abreast again, they faced the river, stamped their feet, nodded their horned heads, swayed their scarlet bodies; they shook towards the fierce river-demon a bunch of black feathers, a mangy skin with a pendent tail—something that looked like a dried gourd; they shouted periodically together strings of amazing words that resembled no sounds of human language; and the deep murmurs of the crowd, interrupted suddenly, were like the responses of some satanic litany.

'We had carried Kurtz into the pilot-house: there was more air there. Lying on the couch, he stared through the open shutter. There was an eddy in the mass of human bodies, and the woman with helmeted head and tawny cheeks rushed out to the very brink of the stream. She put out her hands, shouted something, and all that wild mob took up the shout in a roaring chorus of articulated, rapid, breathless utterance.

'"Do you understand this?" I asked.

'He kept on looking out past me with fiery, longing eyes, with a mingled expression of wistfulness and hate. He made no answer, but I saw a smile, a smile of indefinable meaning, appear on his colourless lips that a moment after twitched convulsively. "Do I not?" he said, slowly, gasping, as if the words had been torn out of him by a supernatural power.

'I pulled the string of the whistle, and I did this because I saw the pilgrims on deck getting out their rifles with an air of anticipating a jolly lark. At the sudden screech there was a movement of abject terror through that wedged mass of bodies. "Don't, don't you frighten them away," cried someone on deck, disconsolately. I pulled the string time after time. They broke and ran, they leaped, they crouched, they swerved, they dodged the flying terror of the sound. The three red chaps had fallen flat, face down on the shore, as though they had been shot dead. Only the barbarous and superb woman did not so much as flinch, and stretched tragically her bare arms after us over the sombre and glittering river.

E

'And then that imbecile crowd down on the deck started their little fun, and I could see nothing more for smoke.

'The brown current ran swiftly out of the heart of darkness, bearing us down towards the sea with twice the speed of our upward progress; and Kurtz's life was running swiftly, too, ebbing, ebbing out of his heart into the sea of inexorable time. The manager was very placid, he had no vital anxieties now, he took us both in with a comprehensive and satisfied glance: the "affair" had come off as well as could be wished. I saw the time approaching when I would be left alone of the party of "unsound method". The pilgrims looked upon me with disfavour. I was, so to speak, numbered with the dead. It is strange how I accepted this unforeseen partnership, this choice of nightmares forced upon me in the tenebrous land invaded by these mean and greedy phantoms.

'Kurtz discoursed. A voice! a voice! It rang deep to the very last. It survived his strength to hide in the magnificent folds of eloquence the barren darkness of his heart. Oh, he struggled! he struggled! The wastes of his weary brain were haunted by shadowy images now—images of wealth and fame revolving obsequiously round his unextinguishable gift of noble and lofty expression. My Intended, my station, my career, my ideas—these were the subjects for the occasional utterances of elevated sentiments. The shade of the original Kurtz frequented the bedside of the hollow sham, whose fate it was to be buried presently in the mould of primeval earth. But both the diabolic love and the unearthly hate of the mysteries it had penetrated fought for the possession of that soul satiated with primitive emotions, avid of lying fame, of sham distinction, of all the appearances of success and power.

'Sometimes he was contemptibly childish. He desired

to have kings meet him at railway stations on his return from some ghastly Nowhere, where he intended to accomplish great things. "You show them you have in you something that is really profitable, and then there will be no limits to the recognition of your ability," he would say. "Of course you must take care of the motives— right motives—always." The long reaches that were like one and the same reach, monotonous bends that were exactly alike, slipped past the steamer with their multitude of secular trees looking patiently after this grimy fragment of another world, the forerunner of change, of conquest, of trade, of massacres, of blessings. I looked ahead—piloting. "Close the shutter," said Kurtz suddenly one day; "I can't bear to look at this." I did so. There was a silence. "Oh, but I will wring your heart yet!" he cried at the invisible wilderness.

'We broke down—as I had expected—and had to lie up for repairs at the head of an island. This delay was the first thing that shook Kurtz's confidence. One morning he gave me a packet of papers and a photograph—the lot tied together with a shoe-string. "Keep this for me," he said. "This noxious fool" (meaning the manager) "is capable of prying into my boxes when I am not looking." In the afternoon I saw him. He was lying on his back with closed eyes, and I withdrew quietly, but I heard him mutter: "Live rightly, die, die . . ." I listened. There was nothing more. Was he rehearsing some speech in his sleep, or was it a fragment of a phrase from some newspaper article? He had been writing for the papers and meant to do so again, "for the furthering of my ideas. It's a duty."

'His was an impenetrable darkness. I looked at him as you peer down at a man who is lying at the bottom of a precipice where the sun never shines. But I had not much time to give him, because I was helping the engine-driver to take to pieces the leaky cylinders, to straighten a bent connecting-rod, and in other such matters. I lived in an infernal mess of rust, filings, nuts, bolts, spanners, hammers, ratchet-drills—things I abominate, because I don't get on with them. I tended the little forge we fortunately had aboard; I toiled wearily in a wretched scrap-heap—unless I had the shakes too bad to stand.

'One evening coming in with a candle I was startled to hear him say a little tremulously: "I am lying here in the dark waiting for death." The light was within a foot of his eyes. I forced myself to murmur, "Oh, nonsense!" and stood over him as if transfixed.

'Anything approaching the change that came over his features I have never seen before, and hope never to see again. Oh, I wasn't touched. I was fascinated. It was as though a veil had been rent. I saw on that ivory face the expression of sombre pride, of ruthless power, of craven terror—of an intense and hopeless despair. Did he live his life again in every detail of desire, temptation, and surrender during that supreme moment of complete knowledge? He cried in a whisper at some image, at some vision—he cried out twice, a cry that was no more than a breath:

'"The horror! The horror!"

'I blew the candle out and left the cabin. The pilgrims were dining in the mess-room, and I took my place opposite the manager, who lifted his eyes to give me a questioning glance, which I successfully ignored. He leaned back, serene, with that peculiar smile of his sealing the unexpressed depths of his meanness. A continuous shower of small flies streamed upon the lamp, upon the cloth, upon our hands and faces. Suddenly the manager's boy put his insolent black head in the doorway, and said in a tone of scathing contempt:

'"Mistah Kurtz—he dead."

'All the pilgrims rushed out to see. I remained, and

went on with my dinner. I believe I was considered brutally callous. However, I did not eat much. There was a lamp in there—light, don't you know—and outside it was so beastly, beastly dark. I went no more near the remarkable man who had pronounced a judgment upon the adventures of his soul on this earth. The voice was gone. What else had been there? But I am of course aware that next day the pilgrims buried something in a muddy hole.

'And then they very nearly buried me.

'However, as you see, I did not go to join Kurtz there and then. I did not. I remained to dream the nightmare out to the end, and to show my loyalty to Kurtz once more. Destiny. My destiny! Droll thing life is—that mysterious arrangement of merciless logic for a futile purpose. The most you can hope from it is some knowledge of yourself—that comes too late—a crop of unextinguishable regrets. I have wrestled with death. It is the most unexciting contest you can imagine. It takes place in an impalpable greyness, with nothing underfoot, with nothing around, without spectators, without clamour, without glory, without the great desire of victory, without the great fear of defeat, in a sickly atmosphere of tepid scepticism, without much belief in your own right, and still less in that of your adversary. If such is the form of ultimate wisdom, then life is a greater riddle than some of us think it to be. I was within a hair's breadth of the last opportunity for pronouncement, and I found with humiliation that probably I would have nothing to say. This is the reason why I affirm that Kurtz was a remarkable man. He had something to say. He said it. Since I had peeped over the edge myself, I understand better the meaning of his stare, that could not see the flame of the candle, but was wide enough to embrace the whole universe, piercing enough to penetrate all the hearts that beat in the darkness.

He had summed up—he had judged. "The horror!" He was a remarkable man. After all, this was the expression of some sort of belief; it had candour, it had conviction, it had a vibrating note of revolt in its whisper, it had the appalling face of a glimpsed truth—the strange commingling of desire and hate. And it is not my own extremity I remember best—a vision of greyness without form filled with physical pain, and a careless contempt for the evanescence of all things—even of this pain itself. No! It is his extremity that I seem to have lived through. True, he had made that last stride, he had stepped over the edge, while I had been permitted to draw back my hesitating foot. And perhaps in this is the whole difference; perhaps all the wisdom, and all truth, and all sincerity, are just compressed into that inappreciable moment of time in which we step over the threshold of the invisible. Perhaps! I like to think my summing-up would not have been a word of careless contempt. Better his cry—much better. It was an affirmation, a moral victory paid for by innumerable defeats, by abominable terrors, by abominable satisfactions. But it was a victory! That is why I have remained loyal to Kurtz to the last, and even beyond, when a long time after I heard once more, not his own voice, but the echo of his magnificent eloquence thrown to me from a soul as translucently pure as a cliff of crystal.

'No, they did not bury me, though there is a period of time which I remember mistily, with a shuddering wonder, like a passage through some inconceivable world that had no hope in it and no desire. I found myself back in the sepulchral city resenting the sight of people hurrying through the streets to filch a little money from each other, to devour their infamous cookery, to gulp their unwholesome beer, to dream their insignificant and silly dreams. They trespassed upon my thoughts. They were intruders whose knowledge of life was to me an irritating pretence,

because I felt so sure they could not possibly know the
things I knew. Their bearing, which was simply the bearing of commonplace individuals going about their business
in the assurance of perfect safety, was offensive to me like
the outrageous flauntings of folly in the face of a danger
it is unable to comprehend. I had no particular desire
to enlighten them, but I had some difficulty in restraining
myself from laughing in their faces, so full of stupid importance. I dare say I was not very well at that time. I
tottered about the streets—there were various affairs to
settle—grinning bitterly at perfectly respectable persons.
I admit my behaviour was inexcusable, but then my
temperature was seldom normal in these days. My dear
aunt's endeavours to "nurse up my strength" seemed
altogether beside the mark. It was not my strength that
wanted nursing, it was my imagination that wanted
soothing. I kept the bundle of papers given me by Kurtz,
not knowing exactly what to do with it. His mother had
died lately, watched over, as I was told, by his Intended.
A clean-shaved man, with an official manner and wearing
gold-rimmed spectacles, called on me one day and made
inquiries, at first circuitous, afterwards suavely pressing,
about what he was pleased to denominate certain "docu-
ments". I was not surprised, because I had had two rows
with the manager on the subject out there. I had refused to
give up the smallest scrap out of that package, and I took
the same attitude with the spectacled man. He became
darkly menacing at last, and with much heat argued that
the Company had the right to every bit of information
about its "territories". And said he: "Mr Kurtz's knowledge of unexplored regions must have been necessarily
extensive and peculiar—owing to his great abilities and to
the deplorable circumstances in which he had been
placed: therefore——" I assured him Mr Kurtz's knowledge, however extensive, did not bear upon the problems

of commerce or administration. He invoked then the name of science. "It would be an incalculable loss if," etc. etc. I offered him the report on the "Suppression of Savage Customs", with the postscriptum torn off. He took it up eagerly, but ended by sniffing at it with an air of contempt. "This is not what we had a right to expect," he remarked. "Expect nothing else," I said. "There are only private letters." He withdrew upon some threat of legal proceedings, and I saw him no more; but another fellow, calling himself Kurtz's cousin, appeared two days later, and was anxious to hear all the details about his dear relative's last moments. Incidentally he gave me to understand that Kurtz had been essentially a great musician. "There was the making of an immense success," said the man, who was an organist, I believe, with lank grey hair flowing over a greasy coat collar. I had no reason to doubt his statement; and to this day I am unable to say what was Kurtz's profession, whether he ever had any—which was the greatest of his talents. I had taken him for a painter who wrote for the papers, or else for a journalist who could paint—but even the cousin (who took snuff during the interview) could not tell me what he had been—exactly. He was a universal genius—on that point I agreed with the old chap, who thereupon blew his nose noisily into a large cotton handkerchief and withdrew in senile agitation, bearing off some family letters and memoranda without importance. Ultimately a journalist anxious to know something of the fate of his "dear colleague" turned up. This visitor informed me Kurtz's proper sphere ought to have been politics "on the popular side". He had furry straight eyebrows, bristly hair cropped short, an eyeglass on a broad ribbon, and, becoming expansive, confessed his opinion that Kurtz really couldn't write a bit—"but heavens! how that man could talk. He electrified large meetings. He had faith—don't you see?—he had the faith. He could get himself to believe anything—anything. He would have been a splendid leader of an extreme party." "What party?" I asked. "Any party," answered the other. "He was an—an—extremist." Did I not think so? I assented. Did I know, he asked, with a sudden flash of curiosity, "what it was that had induced him to go out there?" "Yes," said I, and forthwith handed him the famous Report for publication, if he thought fit. He glanced through it hurriedly, mumbling all the time, judged "it would do", and took himself off with this plunder.

'Thus I was left at last with a slim packet of letters and the girl's portrait. She struck me as beautiful—I mean she had a beautiful expression. I know that the sunlight can be made to lie, too, yet one felt that no manipulation of light and pose could have conveyed the delicate shade of truthfulness upon those features. She seemed ready to listen without mental reservation, without suspicion, without a thought for herself. I concluded I would go and give her back her portrait and those letters myself. Curiosity? Yes; and also some other feeling perhaps. All that had been Kurtz's had passed out of my hands: his soul, his body, his station, his plans, his ivory, his career. There remained only his memory and his Intended—and I wanted to give that up, too, to the past, in a way—to surrender personally all that remained of him with me to that oblivion which is the last word of our common fate. I don't defend myself. I had no clear perception of what it was I really wanted. Perhaps it was an impulse of unconscious loyalty, or the fulfilment of one of these ironic necessities that lurk in the facts of human existence. I don't know. I can't tell. But I went.

'I thought his memory was like the other memories of the dead that accumulate in every man's life—a vague impress on the brain of shadows that had fallen on it in their swift and final passage; but before the high and

*E

ponderous door, between the tall houses of a street as still
and decorous as a well-kept alley in a cemetery, I had a
vision of him on the stretcher, opening his mouth voraci-
ously, as if to devour all the earth with all its mankind.
He lived then before me; he lived as much as he had ever
lived—a shadow insatiable of splendid appearances, of
frightful realities; a shadow darker than the shadow of the
night, and draped nobly in the folds of a gorgeous eloquence. The vision seemed to enter the house with me—
the stretcher, the phantom bearers, the wild crowd of
obedient worshippers, the gloom of the forests, the glitter
of the reach between the murky bends, the beat of the
drum, regular and muffled like the beating of a heart—
the heart of a conquering darkness. It was a moment of
triumph for the wilderness, an invading and vengeful rush
which, it seemed to me, I would have to keep back alone
for the salvation of another soul. And the memory of what
I had heard him say afar there, with the horned shapes
stirring at my back, in the glow of fires, within the patient
woods, those broken phrases came back to me, were heard
again in their ominous and terrifying simplicity. I remembered his abject pleading, his abject threats, the colossal
scale of his vile desires, the meanness, the torment, the
tempestuous anguish of his soul. And later on I seemed to
see his collected languid manner, when he said one day:
"This lot of ivory now is really mine. The Company did
not pay for it. I collected it myself at a very great personal
risk. I am afraid they will try to claim it as theirs though.
H'm. It is a difficult case. What do you think I ought to
do—resist? Eh? I want no more than justice." . . . He
wanted no more than justice—no more than justice. I
rang the bell before a mahogany door on the first floor,
and while I waited he seemed to stare at me out of the
glassy panel—stare with that wide and immense stare
embracing, condemning, loathing all the universe. I

seemed to hear the whispered cry: "The horror! The horror!"

'The dusk was falling. I had to wait in a lofty drawing-room with three long windows from floor to ceiling that were like three luminous and bedraped columns. The bent gilt legs and backs of the furniture shone in indistinct curves. The tall marble fireplace had a cold and monumental whiteness. A grand piano stood massively in a corner; with dark gleams on the flat surfaces like a sombre and polished sarcophagus. A high door opened—closed. I rose.

'She came forward, all in black, with a pale head, floating towards me in the dusk. She was in mourning. It was more than a year since his death, more than a year since the news came; she seemed as though she would remember and mourn for ever. She took both my hands in hers and murmured: "I had heard you were coming." I noticed she was not very young—I mean not girlish. She had a mature capacity for fidelity, for belief, for suffering. The room seemed to have grown darker, as if all the sad light of the cloudy evening had taken refuge on her forehead. This fair hair, this pale visage, this pure brow, seemed surrounded by an ashy halo from which the dark eyes looked out at me. Their glance was guileless, profound, confident, and trustful. She carried her sorrowful head as though she were proud of that sorrow, as though she would say, I—I alone know how to mourn for him as he deserves. But while we were still shaking hands, such a look of awful desolation came upon her face that I perceived she was one of those creatures that are not the playthings of Time. For her he had died only yesterday. And, by Jove! the impression was so powerful that for me, too, he seemed to have died only yesterday—nay, this very minute. I saw her and him in the same instant of time—his death and her sorrow—I saw her sorrow in the very moment of his death. Do you understand? I saw them together—I heard them together. She had said, with a deep catch of the breath, "I have survived", while my strained ears seemed to hear distinctly, mingled with her tone of despairing regret, the summing-up whisper of his eternal condemnation. I asked myself what I was doing there, with a sensation of panic in my heart as though I had blundered into a place of cruel and absurd mysteries not fit for a human being to behold. She motioned me to a chair. We sat down. I laid the packet gently on the little table, and she put her hand over it. . . . "You knew him well," she murmured, after a moment of mourning silence.

"'Intimacy grows quickly out there," I said. "I knew him as well as it is possible for one man to know another."

"'And you admired him," she said. "It was impossible to know him and not to admire him. Was it?"

"'He was a remarkable man," I said, unsteadily. Then before the appealing fixity of her gaze, that seemed to watch for more words on my lips, I went on: "It was impossible not to——"

"'Love him," she finished eagerly, silencing me into an appalled dumbness. "How true! how true! But when you think that no one knew him so well as I! I had all his noble confidence. I knew him best."

"'You knew him best," I repeated. And perhaps she did. But with every word spoken the room was growing darker, and only her forehead, smooth and white, remained illumined by the unextinguishable light of belief and love.

"'You were his friend," she went on. "His friend," she repeated, a little louder. "You must have been, if he had given you this, and sent you to me. I feel I can speak to you—and oh, I must speak. I want you—you who have heard his last words—to know I have been worthy of him. . . . It is not pride. . . . Yes! I am proud to know I understood him better than anyone on earth—he told me so himself. And since his mother died I have had no one— no one—to—to——"

'I listened. The darkness deepened. I was not even sure whether he had given me the right bundle. I rather suspect he wanted me to take care of another batch of his papers which, after his death, I saw the manager examining under the lamp. And the girl talked, easing her pain in the certitude of my sympathy; she talked as thirsty men drink. I had heard that her engagement with Kurtz had been disapproved by her people. He wasn't rich enough or something. And indeed I don't know whether he had not been a pauper all his life. He had given me some reason to infer that it was his impatience of comparative poverty that drove him out there.

'". . . Who was not his friend who had heard him speak once?" she was saying. "He drew men towards him by what was best in them." She looked at me with intensity. "It is the gift of the great," she went on, and the sound of her low voice seemed to have the accompaniment of all the other sounds, full of mystery, desolation, and sorrow, I had ever heard—the ripple of the river, the soughing of the trees swayed by the wind, the murmurs of the crowds, the faint ring of incomprehensible words cried from afar, the whisper of a voice speaking from beyond the threshold of an eternal darkness. "But you have heard him! You know!" she cried.

'"Yes, I know," I said with something like despair in my heart, but bowing my head before the faith that was in her, before that great and saving illusion that shone with an unearthly glow in the darkness, in the triumphant darkness from which I could not have defended her— from which I could not even defend myself.

'"What a loss to me—to us!" she corrected herself with beautiful generosity; then added in a murmur: "To the world." By the last gleams of twilight I could see the glitter of her eyes, full of tears—of tears that would not fall.

'"I have been very happy—very fortunate—very proud," she went on. "Too fortunate. Too happy for a little while. And now I am unhappy for—for life."

'She stood up; her fair hair seemed to catch all the remaining light in a glimmer of gold. I rose, too.

'"And of all this," she went on, mournfully, "of all his promise, and of all his greatness, of his generous mind, of his noble heart, nothing remains—nothing but a memory. You and I——"

'"We shall always remember him," I said, hastily.

'"No!" she cried. "It is impossible that all this should be lost—that such a life should be sacrificed to leave nothing—but sorrow. You know what vast plans he had. I knew of them, too—I could not perhaps understand—but others knew of them. Something must remain. His words, at least, have not died."

'"His words will remain," I said.

'"And his example," she whispered to herself. "Men looked up to him—his goodness shone in every act. His example——"

'"True," I said; "his example, too. Yes, his example. I forgot that."

'"But I do not. I cannot—I cannot believe—not yet. I cannot believe that I shall never see him again, that nobody will see him again, never, never, never."

'She put out her arms as if after a retreating figure, stretching them black and with clasped pale hands across the fading and narrow sheen of the window. Never see him! I saw him clearly enough then. I shall see this eloquent phantom as long as I live, and I shall see her, too, a tragic and familiar Shade, resembling in this gesture another one, tragic also, and bedecked with powerless charms, stretching bare brown arms over the glitter of the infernal stream, the stream of darkness. She said suddenly very low: "He died as he lived."

"'His end", said I, with dull anger stirring in me, "was in every way worthy of his life."

"'And I was not with him," she murmured. My anger subsided before a feeling of infinite pity.

"'Everything that could be done——" I mumbled.

"'Ah, but I believed in him more than anyone on earth —more than his own mother, more than—himself. He needed me! Me! I would have treasured every sigh, every word, every sign, every glance."

'I felt like a chill grip on my chest. "Don't," I said, in a muffled voice.

"'Forgive me. I—I—have mourned so long in silence— in silence. . . . You were with him—to the last? I think of his loneliness. Nobody near to understand him as I would have understood. Perhaps no one to hear. . . ."

"'To the very end," I said, shakily. "I heard his very last words——" I stopped in a fright.

"'Repeat them," she murmured in a heart-broken tone. "I want—I want—something—something—to—to live with."

'I was on the point of crying at her, "Don't you hear them?" The dusk was repeating them in a persistent whisper all around us, in a whisper that seemed to swell menacingly like the first whisper of a rising wind. "The horror! The horror!"

"'His last word—to live with," she insisted. "Don't you understand I loved him—I loved him—I loved him!"

'I pulled myself together and spoke slowly.

"'The last word he pronounced was—your name."

'I heard a light sigh and then my heart stood still, stopped dead short by an exulting and terrible cry, by the cry of inconceivable triumph and of unspeakable pain. "I knew it—I was sure!" . . . She knew. She was sure. I heard her weeping; she had hidden her face in her hands. It seemed to me that the house would collapse before I could escape, that the heavens would fall upon my head. But nothing happened. The heavens do not fall for such a trifle. Would they have fallen, I wonder, if I had rendered Kurtz that justice which was his due? Hadn't he said he wanted only justice? But I couldn't. I could not tell her. It would have been too dark—too dark altogether. . . .'

Marlow ceased, and sat apart, indistinct and silent, in the pose of a meditating Buddha. Nobody moved for a time. 'We have lost the first of the ebb,' said the Director, suddenly. I raised my head. The offing was barred by a black bank of clouds, and the tranquil waterway leading to the uttermost ends of the earth flowed sombre under an overcast sky—seemed to lead into the heart of an immense darkness.

AN OUTPOST OF PROGRESS

AN OUTPOST OF PROGRESS

I

THERE were two white men in charge of the trading station. Kayerts, the chief, was short and fat; Carlier, the assistant, was tall, with a large head and a very broad trunk perched upon a long pair of thin legs. The third man on the staff was a Sierra Leone negro, who maintained that his name was Henry Price. However, for some reason or other, the natives down the river had given him the name of Makola, and it stuck to him through all his wanderings about the country. He spoke English and French with a warbling accent, wrote a beautiful hand, understood book-keeping, and cherished in his innermost heart the worship of Evil Spirits. His wife was a negress from Loanda, very large and very noisy. Three children rolled about in sunshine before the door of his low, shed-like dwelling. Makola, taciturn and impenetrable, despised the two white men. He had charge of a small clay store-house with a dried-grass roof, and pretended to keep a correct account of beads, cotton cloth, red kerchiefs, brass wire, and other trade goods it contained. Besides the storehouse and Makola's hut, there was only one large building in the cleared ground of the station. It was built neatly of reeds, with a veranda on all the four sides. There were three rooms in it. The one in the middle was the

117

living-room, and had two rough tables and a few stools in it. The other two were the bedrooms for the white men. Each had a bedstead and a mosquito net for all furniture. The plank floor was littered with the belongings of the white men; open half-empty boxes, town wearing apparel, old boots; all the things dirty, and all the things broken, that accumulate mysteriously round untidy men. There was also another dwelling-place some distance away from the buildings. In it, under a tall cross much out of the perpendicular, slept the man who had seen the beginning of all this; who had planned and had watched the construction of this outpost of progress. He had been, at home, an unsuccessful painter who, weary of pursuing fame on an empty stomach, had gone out there through high protections. He had been the first chief of that station. Makola had watched the energetic artist die of fever in the just finished house with his usual kind of 'I told you so' indifference. Then, for a time, he dwelt alone with his family, his account books, and the Evil Spirit that rules the lands under the equator. He got on very well with his god. Perhaps he had propitiated him by a promise of more white men to play with, by and by. At any rate the director of the Great Trading Company, coming up in a steamer that resembled an enormous sardine box with a flat-roofed shed erected on it, found the station in good order, and Makola as usual quietly diligent. The director had the cross put up over the first agent's grave, and appointed Kayerts to the post. Carlier was told off as second in charge. The director was a man ruthless and efficient, who at times, but very imperceptibly, indulged in grim humour. He made a speech to Kayerts and Carlier, pointing out to them the promising aspect of their station. The nearest trading-post was about three hundred miles away. It was an exceptional opportunity for them to distinguish themselves and to earn percentages on the trade. This appointment was a favour done to beginners. Kayerts was moved almost to tears by his director's kindness. He would, he said, by doing his best, try to justify the flattering confidence, etc. etc. Kayerts had been in the Administration of the Telegraphs, and knew how to express himself correctly. Carlier, an ex-non-commissioned officer of cavalry in an army guaranteed from harm by several European powers, was less impressed. If there were commissions to get, so much the better; and, trailing a sulky glance over the river, the forests, the impenetrable bush that seemed to cut off the station from the rest of the world, he muttered between his teeth: 'We shall see, very soon.'

Next day, some bales of cotton goods and a few cases of provisions having been thrown on shore, the sardine-box steamer went off, not to return for another six months. On the deck the director touched his cap to the two agents, who stood on the bank waving their hats, and, turning to an old servant of the Company on his passage to head-quarters, said: 'Look at those two imbeciles. They must be mad at home to send me such specimens. I told those fellows to plant a vegetable garden, build new storehouses and fences, and construct a landing-stage. I bet nothing will be done! They won't know how to begin. I always thought the station on this river useless, and they just fit the station!'

'They will form themselves there,' said the old stager with a quiet smile.

'At any rate, I am rid of them for six months,' retorted the director.

The two men watched the steamer round the bend, then, ascending arm in arm the slope of the bank, returned to the station. They had been in this vast and dark country only a very short time, and as yet always in the midst of other white men, under the eye and guidance of their superiors. And now, dull as they were to the subtle influences of surroundings, they felt themselves very much alone, when suddenly left unassisted to face the wilderness; a wilderness rendered more strange, more incomprehensible by the mysterious glimpses of the vigorous life it contained. They were two perfectly insignificant and incapable individuals, whose existence is only rendered possible through the high organization of civilized crowds. Few men realize that their life, the very essence of their character, their capabilities and their audacities, are only the expression of their belief in the safety of their surroundings. The courage, the composure, the confidence; the emotions and principles; every great and every insignificant thought belongs not to the individual but to the crowd: to the crowd that believes blindly in the irresistible force of its institutions and of its morals, in the power of its police and of its opinion. But the contact with pure unmitigated savagery, with primitive nature and primitive man, brings sudden and profound trouble into the heart. To the sentiment of being alone of one's kind, to the clear perception of the loneliness of one's thoughts, of one's sensations—to the negation of the habitual, which is safe, there is added the affirmation of the unusual, which is dangerous; a suggestion of things vague, uncontrollable, and repulsive, whose discomposing intrusion excites the imagination and tries the civilized nerves of the foolish and the wise alike.

Kayerts and Carlier walked arm in arm, drawing close to one another as children do in the dark; and they had the same, not altogether unpleasant, sense of danger which one half suspects to be imaginary. They chatted persistently in familiar tones. 'Our station is prettily situated,' said one. The other assented with enthusiasm, enlarging volubly on the beauties of the situation. Then they passed near the grave. 'Poor devil!' said Kayerts. 'He died of fever, didn't he?' muttered Carlier, stopping short. 'Why,' retorted Kayerts, with indignation, 'I've been told that the fellow exposed himself recklessly to the sun. The climate here, everybody says, is not at all worse than at home, as long as you keep out of the sun. Do you hear that, Carlier? I am chief here, and my orders are that you should not expose yourself to the sun!' He assumed his superiority jocularly, but his meaning was serious. The idea that he would, perhaps, have to bury Carlier and remain alone, gave him an inward shiver. He felt suddenly that this Carlier was more precious to him here, in the centre of Africa, than a brother could be anywhere else. Carlier, entering into the spirit of the thing, made a military salute and answered in a brisk tone: 'Your orders shall be attended to, chief!' Then he burst out laughing, slapped Kayerts on the back and shouted: 'We shall let life run easily here! Just sit still and gather in the ivory those savages will bring. This country has its good points, after all!' They both laughed loudly, while Carlier thought: 'That poor Kayerts; he is so fat and unhealthy. It would be awful if I had to bury him here. He is a man I respect. . . .' Before they reached the veranda of their house they called one another 'my dear fellow'.

The first day they were very active, pottering about with hammers and nails and red calico, to put up curtains, make their house habitable and pretty; resolved to settle down comfortably to their new life. For them an impossible task. To grapple effectually with even purely material problems requires more serenity of mind and more lofty courage than people generally imagine. No two beings could have been more unfitted for such a struggle. Society, not from any tenderness, but because of its strange needs, had taken care of those two men, forbidding them all independent thought, all initiative, all departure from routine; and forbidding it under pain of death. They could only live on condition of being machines. And now, released from the fostering care of men with pens behind the ears, or of men with gold lace on the sleeves, they were like those lifelong prisoners who, liberated after many years, do not know what use to make of their freedom. They did not know what use to make of their faculties, being both, through want of practice, incapable of independent thought.

At the end of two months Kayerts often would say: 'If it was not for my Melie, you wouldn't catch me here.' Melie was his daughter. He had thrown up his post in the Administration of the Telegraphs, though he had been for seventeen years perfectly happy there, to earn a dowry for his girl. His wife was dead, and the child was being brought up by his sisters. He regretted the streets, the pavements, the cafés, his friends of many years; all the things he used to see, day after day; all the thoughts suggested by familiar things—the thoughts effortless, monotonous, and soothing of a Government clerk; he regretted all the gossip, the small enmities, the mild venom, and the little jokes of Government offices. 'If I had had a decent brother-in-law,' Carlier would remark, 'a fellow with a heart, I would not be here.' He had left the army and had made himself so obnoxious to his family by his laziness and impudence that an exasperated brother-in-law had made superhuman efforts to procure him an appointment in the Company as a second-class agent. Having not a penny in the world he was compelled to accept this means of livelihood as soon as it became quite clear to him that there was nothing more to squeeze out of his relations. He, like Kayerts, regretted his old life. He regretted the clink of sabre and spurs on a fine afternoon, the barrack-room witticisms, the girls of garrison towns; but, besides, he had also a sense of grievance. He was evidently a much ill-used man. This made him moody at times. But the two men got on well together in the fellowship of their stupidity and laziness. Together they did nothing, absolutely nothing, and enjoyed the sense of idleness for which they were paid. And in time they came to feel something resembling affection for one another.

They lived like blind men in a large room, aware only of what came in contact with them (and of that only imperfectly), but unable to see the general aspect of things. The river, the forest, all the great land throbbing with life, were like a great emptiness. Even the brilliant sunshine disclosed nothing intelligible. Things appeared and disappeared before their eyes in an unconnected and aimless kind of way. The river seemed to come from nowhere and flow nowhither. It flowed through a void. Out of that void, at times, came canoes, and men with spears in their hands would suddenly crowd the yard of the station. They were naked, glossy black, ornamented with snowy shells and glistening brass wire, perfect of limb. They made an uncouth babbling noise when they spoke, moved in a stately manner, and sent quick, wild glances out of their startled, never-resting eyes. Those warriors would squat in long rows, four or more deep, before the veranda, while their chiefs bargained for hours with Makola over an elephant tusk. Kayerts sat on his chair and looked down on the proceedings, understanding nothing. He stared at them with his round blue eyes, called out to Carlier: 'Here, look! Look at that fellow there—and that other one, to the left. Did you ever see such a face? Oh, the funny brute!'

Carlier, smoking native tobacco in a short wooden pipe, would swagger up twirling his moustaches and, surveying the warriors with haughty indulgence, would say:

'Fine animals. Brought any bone? Yes? It's not any too soon. Look at the muscles of that fellow—third from the end. I wouldn't care to get a punch on the nose from him. Fine arms, but legs no good below the knee. Couldn't make cavalrymen of them.' And after glancing down complacently at his own shanks, he always concluded: 'Pah! Don't they stink! You, Makola! Take that herd over to the fetish' (the storehouse was in every station called the fetish, perhaps because of the spirit of civilization it contained) 'and give them up some of the rubbish you keep there. I'd rather see it full of bone than full of rags.'

Kayerts approved.

'Yes, yes! Go and finish that palaver over there, Mr Makola. I will come round when you are ready, to weigh the tusk. We must be careful.' Then turning to his companion: 'This is the tribe that lives down the river; they are rather aromatic. I remember, they had been once before here. D'ye hear that row? What a fellow has got to put up with in this dog of a country! My head is split.'

Such profitable visits were rare. For days the two pioneers of trade and progress would look on their empty courtyard in the vibrating brilliance of vertical sunshine. Below the high bank, the silent river flowed on glittering and steady. On the sands in the middle of the stream, hippos and alligators sunned themselves side by side. And stretching away in all directions, surrounding the insignificant cleared spot of the trading-post, immense forests, hiding fateful complications of fantastic life, lay in the eloquent silence of mute greatness. The two men understood nothing, cared for nothing but for the passage of days that separated them from the steamer's return. Their predecessor had left some torn books. They took up these wrecks of novels, and, as they had never read anything of the kind before, they were surprised and amused. Then during long days there were interminable and silly discussions about plots and personages. In the centre of Africa they made acquaintance of Richelieu and of d'Artagnan, of Hawk's Eye and of Father Goriot, and of many other people. All these imaginary personages became subjects for gossip as if they had been living friends. They discounted their virtues, suspected their motives, decried their successes; were scandalized at their duplicity or were doubtful about their courage. The accounts of crimes filled them with indignation, while tender or pathetic passages moved them deeply. Carlier cleared his throat and said in a soldierly voice: 'What nonsense!' Kayerts, his round eyes suffused with tears, his fat cheeks quivering, rubbed his bald head and declared: 'This is a splendid book. I had no idea there were such clever fellows in the world.' They also found some old copies of a home paper. That print discussed what it was pleased to call 'Our Colonial Expansion' in high-flown language. It spoke much of the rights and duties of civilization, of the sacredness of the civilizing work, and extolled the merits of those who went about bringing light and faith and commerce to the dark places of the earth. Carlier and Kayerts read, wondered, and began to think better of themselves. Carlier said one evening, waving his hand about: 'In a hundred years there will be perhaps a town here. Quays and warehouses and barracks and—and—billiard-rooms. Civilization, my boy, and virtue—and all. And then, chaps will read that two good fellows, Kayerts and Carlier, were the first civilized men to live in this very spot!' Kayerts nodded: 'Yes, it is a consolation to think of that.' They seemed to forget their dead predecessor; but, early one day, Carlier went out and replanted the cross firmly. 'It used to make me squint whenever I walked that way,' he explained to Kayerts over the morning coffee. 'It made me squint, leaning over so much. So I just planted it upright. And solid, I promise you! I suspended myself with both hands to the cross-piece. Not a move. Oh, I did that properly.'

At times Gobila came to see them. Gobila was the chief of the neighbouring villages. He was a grey-headed savage, thin and black, with a white cloth round his loins and a mangy panther skin hanging over his back. He came up with long strides of his skeleton legs, swinging a staff as tall as himself, and, entering the common room of the station, would squat on his heels to the left of the door. There he sat, watching Kayerts, and now and then making a speech which the other did not understand. Kayerts, without interrupting his occupation, would from time to time say in a friendly manner, 'How goes it, you old image?' and they would smile at one another. The two whites had a liking for that old and incomprehensible creature, and called him Father Gobila. Gobila's manner was paternal, and he seemed really to love all white men. They all appeared to him very young, indistinguishably alike (except for stature), and he knew that they were all brothers, and also immortal. The death of the artist, who was the first white man whom he knew intimately, did not disturb this belief, because he was firmly convinced that the white stranger had pretended to die and got himself buried for some mysterious purpose of his own, into which it was useless to inquire. Perhaps it was his way of going home to his own country? At any rate, these were his brothers, and he transferred his absurd affection to them. They returned it in a way. Carlier slapped him on the back, and recklessly struck off matches for his amusement. Kayerts was always ready to let him have a sniff at the ammonia bottle. In short, they behaved just like that other white creature that had hidden itself in a hole in the ground. Gobila considered them attentively. Perhaps they were the same being with the other—or one of them was. He couldn't decide—clear up that mystery; but he remained always very friendly. In consequence of that friendship the women of Gobila's village walked in single file through the reedy grass, bringing every morning to the station fowls and sweet potatoes and palm wine, and sometimes a goat. The Company never provisions the stations fully, and the agents required those local supplies to live. They had them through the goodwill of Gobila, and lived well. Now and then one of them had a bout of fever, and the other nursed him with gentle devotion. They did not think much of it. It left them weaker, and their appearance changed for the worse. Carlier was hollow-eyed and irritable. Kayerts showed a drawn, flabby face above the rotundity of his stomach, which gave him a weird aspect. But being constantly together, they did not notice the change that took place gradually in their appearance, and also in their dispositions.

Five months passed in that way.

Then, one morning, as Kayerts and Carlier, lounging in their chairs under the veranda, talked about the approaching visit of the steamer, a knot of armed men came out of the forest and advanced towards the station. They were strangers to that part of the country. They were tall, slight, draped classically from neck to heel in blue fringed cloths, and carried percussion muskets over their bare right shoulders. Makola showed signs of excitement, and ran out of the storehouse (where he spent all his days) to meet these visitors. They came into the courtyard and looked about them with steady, scornful glances. Their leader, a powerful and determined-looking negro with bloodshot eyes, stood in front of the veranda and made a long speech. He gesticulated much, and ceased very suddenly.

There was something in his intonation, in the sounds of the long sentences he used, that startled the two whites.

It was like a reminiscence of something not exactly familiar, and yet resembling the speech of civilized men. It sounded like one of those impossible languages which sometimes we hear in our dreams.

'What lingo is that?' said the amazed Carlier. 'In the first moment I fancied the fellow was going to speak French. Anyway, it is a different kind of gibberish to what we ever heard.'

'Yes,' replied Kayerts. 'Hey, Makola, what does he say? Where do they come from? Who are they?'

But Makola, who seemed to be standing on hot bricks, answered hurriedly: 'I don't know. They come from very far. Perhaps Mrs Price will understand. They are perhaps bad men.'

The leader, after waiting for a while, said something sharply to Makola, who shook his head. Then the man, after looking round, noticed Makola's hut and walked over there. The next moment Mrs Makola was heard speaking with great volubility. The other strangers—they were six in all—strolled about with an air of ease, put their heads through the door of the storeroom, congregated round the grave, pointed understandingly at the cross, and generally made themselves at home.

'I don't like those chaps—and, I say, Kayerts, they must be from the coast; they've got firearms,' observed the sagacious Carlier.

Kayerts also did not like those chaps. They both, for the first time, became aware that they lived in conditions where the unusual may be dangerous, and that there was no power on earth outside of themselves to stand between them and the unusual. They became uneasy, went in and loaded their revolvers. Kayerts said: 'We must order Makola to tell them to go away before dark.'

The strangers left in the afternoon, after eating a meal prepared for them by Mrs Makola. The immense woman was excited, and talked much with the visitors. She rattled away shrilly, pointing here and there at the forests and at the river. Makola sat apart and watched. At times he got up and whispered to his wife. He accompanied the strangers across the ravine at the back of the station ground, and returned slowly looking very thoughtful. When questioned by the white men he was very strange, seemed not to understand, seemed to have forgotten French—seemed to have forgotten how to speak altogether. Kayerts and Carlier agreed that the negro had had too much palm wine.

There was some talk about keeping a watch in turn, but in the evening everything seemed so quiet and peaceful that they retired as usual. All night they were disturbed by a lot of drumming in the villages. A deep, rapid roll near by would be followed by another far off—then all ceased. Soon short appeals would rattle out here and there, then all mingle together, increase, become vigorous and sustained, would spread out over the forest, roll through the night, unbroken and ceaseless, near and far, as if the whole land had been one immense drum booming out steadily an appeal to heaven. And through the deep and tremendous noise sudden yells that resembled snatches of songs from a madhouse darted shrill and high in discordant jets of sound which seemed to rush far above the earth and drive all peace from under the stars.

Carlier and Kayerts slept badly. They both thought they had heard shots fired during the night—but they could not agree as to the direction. In the morning Makola was gone somewhere. He returned about noon with one of yesterday's strangers, and eluded all Kayerts's attempts to close with him: had become deaf apparently. Kayerts wondered. Carlier, who had been fishing off the bank, came back and remarked while he showed his catch: 'The negroes seem to be in a deuce of a stir; I wonder what's up. I saw about fifteen canoes cross the river during the two hours I was there fishing.' Kayerts, worried, said: 'Isn't this Makola very queer today?' Carlier advised: 'Keep all our men together in case of some trouble.'

II

THERE were ten station men who had been left by the director. Those fellows, having engaged themselves to the Company for six months (without having any idea of a month in particular and only a very faint notion of time in general), had been serving the cause of progress for upwards of two years. Belonging to a tribe from a very distant part of the land of darkness and sorrow, they did not run away, naturally supposing that as wandering strangers they would be killed by the inhabitants of the country; in which they were right. They lived in straw huts on the slope of a ravine overgrown with reedy grass, just behind the station buildings. They were not happy, regretting the festive incantations, the sorceries, the human sacrifices of their own land; where they also had parents, brothers, sisters, admired chiefs, respected magicians, loved friends, and other ties supposed generally to be human. Besides, the rice rations served out by the Company did not agree with them, being a food unknown to their land, and to which they could not get used. Consequently they were unhealthy and miserable. Had they been of any other tribe they would have made up their minds to die—for nothing is easier to certain savages than suicide—and so have escaped from the puzzling difficulties of existence. But belonging, as they did, to a warlike tribe with filed teeth, they had more grit, and went on stupidly

F　　　　　　　131

living through disease and sorrow. They did very little work, and had lost their splendid physique. Carlier and Kayerts doctored them assiduously without being able to bring them back into condition again. They were mustered every morning and told off to different tasks—grass-cutting, fence-building, tree-felling, etc. etc., which no power on earth could induce them to execute efficiently. The two whites had practically very little control over them.

In the afternoon Makola came over to the big house and found Kayerts watching three heavy columns of smoke rising above the forests. 'What is that?' asked Kayerts. 'Some villages burn,' answered Makola, who seemed to have regained his wits. Then he said abruptly: 'We have got very little ivory; bad six months' trading. Do you like get a little more ivory?'

'Yes,' said Kayerts, eagerly. He thought of percentages which were low.

'Those men who came yesterday are traders from Loanda who have got more ivory than they can carry home. Shall I buy? I know their camp.'

'Certainly,' said Kayerts. 'What are those traders?'

'Bad fellows,' said Makola, indifferently. 'They fight with people, and catch women and children. They are bad men, and got guns. There is a great disturbance in the country. Do you want ivory?'

'Yes,' said Kayerts. Makola said nothing for a while. Then: 'Those workmen of ours are no good at all,' he muttered, looking round. 'Station in very bad order, sir. Director will growl. Better get a fine lot of ivory, then he say nothing.'

'I can't help it; the men won't work,' said Kayerts. 'When will you get that ivory?'

'Very soon,' said Makola. 'Perhaps tonight. You leave it to me, and keep indoors, sir. I think you had better give some palm wine to our men to make a dance this evening. Enjoy themselves. Work better tomorrow. There's plenty palm wine—gone a little sour.'

Kayerts said yes, and Makola, with his own hands, carried big calabashes to the door of his hut. They stood there till the evening, and Mrs Makola looked into every one. The men got them at sunset. When Kayerts and Carlier retired, a big bonfire was flaring before the men's huts. They could hear their shouts and drumming. Some men from Gobila's village had joined the station hands, and the entertainment was a great success.

In the middle of the night Carlier, waking suddenly, heard a man shout loudly; then a shot was fired. Only one. Carlier ran out and met Kayerts on the veranda. They were both startled. As they went across the yard to call Makola, they saw shadows moving in the night. One of them cried: 'Don't shoot! It's me, Price.' Then Makola appeared close to them. 'Go back, go back, please,' he urged, 'you spoil all.' 'There are strange men about,' said Carlier. 'Never mind; I know,' said Makola. Then he whispered: 'All right. Bring ivory. Say nothing! I know my business.' The two white men reluctantly went back to the house, but did not sleep. They heard footsteps, whispers, some groans. It seemed as if a lot of men came in, dumped heavy things on the ground, squabbled a long time, then went away. They lay on their hard beds and thought: 'This Makola is invaluable.' In the morning Carlier came out, very sleepy, and pulled at the cord of the big bell. The station hands mustered every morning to the sound of the bell. That morning nobody came. Kayerts turned out also, yawning. Across the yard they saw Makola come out of his hut, a tin basin of soapy water in his hand. Makola, a civilized negro, was very neat in his person. He threw the soapsuds skilfully over a wretched little yellow cur he had, then turning his face to the agent's house, he shouted from the distance: 'All the men gone last night!'

They heard him plainly, but in their surprise they both yelled out together: 'What!' Then they stared at one another. 'We are in a proper fix now,' growled Carlier. 'It's incredible!' muttered Kayerts. 'I will go to the huts and see,' said Carlier, striding off. Makola coming up found Kayerts standing alone.

'I can hardly believe it,' said Kayerts, tearfully. 'We took care of them as if they had been our children.'

'They went with the coast people,' said Makola after a moment of hesitation.

'What do I care with whom they went—the ungrateful brutes!' exclaimed the other. Then with sudden suspicion, and looking hard at Makola, he added: 'What do you know about it?'

Makola moved his shoulders, looking down on the ground. 'What do I know? I think only. Will you come and look at the ivory I've got there? It is a fine lot. You never saw such.'

He moved towards the store. Kayerts followed him mechanically, thinking about the incredible desertion of the men. On the ground before the door of the fetish lay six splendid tusks.

'What did you give for it?' asked Kayerts, after surveying the lot with satisfaction.

'No regular trade,' said Makola. 'They brought the ivory and gave it to me. I told them to take what they most wanted in the station. It is a beautiful lot. No station can show such tusks. Those traders wanted carriers badly, and our men were no good here. No trade, no entry in books; all correct.'

Kayerts nearly burst with indignation. 'Why,' he shouted, 'I believe you have sold our men for these tusks!' Makola stood impassive and silent.

'I—I—will—I . . .,' stuttered Kayerts. 'You fiend!' he yelled out.

'I did the best for you and the Company,' said Makola, imperturbably. 'Why you shout so much? Look at this tusk.'

'I dismiss you! I will report you—I won't look at the tusk. I forbid you to touch them. I order you to throw them into the river. You—you!'

'You very red, Mr Kayerts. If you are so irritable in the sun, you will get fever and die—like the first chief!' pronounced Makola, impressively.

They stood still, contemplating one another with intense eyes, as if they had been looking with effort across immense distances. Kayerts shivered. Makola had meant no more than he said, but his words seemed to Kayerts full of ominous menace. He turned sharply and went away to the house. Makola retired into the bosom of his family; and the tusks, left lying before the store, looked very large and valuable in the sunshine.

Carlier came back on the veranda. 'They're all gone, hey?' asked Kayerts from the far end of the common room in a muffled voice. 'You did not find anybody?'

'Oh yes,' said Carlier, 'I found one of Gobila's people lying dead before the huts—shot through the body. We heard that shot last night.'

Kayerts came out quickly. He found his companion staring grimly over the yard at the tusks, away by the store. They both sat in silence for a while. Then Kayerts related his conversation with Makola. Carlier said nothing. At the midday meal they ate very little. They hardly exchanged a word that day. A great silence seemed to lie heavily over the station and press on their lips. Makola did not open the store; he spent the day playing with his children. He lay full length on a mat outside his door, and the youngsters sat on his chest and clambered all over him.

It was a touching picture. Mrs Makola was busy cooking all day as usual. The white men made a somewhat better meal in the evening. Afterwards Carlier, smoking his pipe, strolled over to the store; he stood for a long time over the tusks, touched one or two with his foot, even tried to lift the largest one by its small end. He came back to his chief, who had not stirred from the veranda, threw himself in the chair and said:

'I can see it! They were pounced upon while they slept heavily after drinking all that palm wine you've allowed Makola to give them. A put-up job! See? The worst is, some of Gobila's people were there, and got carried off too, no doubt. The least drunk woke up, and got shot for his sobriety. This is a funny country. What will you do now?'

'We can't touch it, of course,' said Kayerts.

'Of course not,' assented Carlier.

'Slavery is an awful thing,' stammered out Kayerts in an unsteady voice.

'Frightful—the sufferings,' grunted Carlier with conviction.

They believed their words. Everybody shows a respectful deference to certain sounds that he and his fellows can make. But about feelings people really know nothing. We talk with indignation or enthusiasm; we talk about oppression, cruelty, crime, devotion, self-sacrifice, virtue, and we know nothing real beyond the words. Nobody knows what suffering or sacrifice mean—except perhaps the victims of the mysterious purpose of these illusions.

Next morning they saw Makola very busy setting up in the yard the big scales used for weighing ivory. By and by Carlier said, 'What's that filthy scoundrel up to?' and lounged out into the yard. Kayerts followed. They stood watching. Makola took no notice. When the balance was swung true, he tried to lift a tusk into the scale. It was too heavy. He looked up helplessly without a word, and for a minute they stood round that balance as mute and still as three statues. Suddenly Carlier said, 'Catch hold of the other end, Makola—you beast!' and together they swung the tusk up. Kayerts trembled in every limb. He muttered, 'I say! Oh, I say!' and putting his hand in his pocket found there a dirty bit of paper and the stump of a pencil. He turned his back on the others, as if about to do something tricky, and noted stealthily the weights which Carlier shouted out to him with unnecessary loudness. When all was over Makola whispered to himself: 'The sun's very strong here for the tusks.' Carlier said to Kayerts in a careless tone: 'I say, chief, I might just as well give him a lift with this lot into the store.'

As they were going back to the house Kayerts observed with a sigh: 'It had to be done.' And Carlier said: 'It's deplorable, but the men being Company's men the ivory is Company's ivory. We must look after it.' 'I will report to the director, of course,' said Kayerts. 'Of course; let him decide,' approved Carlier.

At midday they made a hearty meal. Kayerts sighed from time to time. Whenever they mentioned Makola's name they always added to it an approbrious epithet. It eased their conscience. Makola gave himself a half-holiday, and bathed his children in the river. No one from Gobila's villages came near the station that day. No one came the next day, and the next, nor for a whole week. Gobila's people might have been dead and buried for any sign of life they gave. But they were only mourning for those they had lost by the witchcraft of white men, who had brought wicked people into their country. The wicked people were gone, but fear remained. Fear always remains. A man may destroy everything within himself, love and hate and belief, and even doubt; but as long as he clings to life he cannot destroy fear: the fear, subtle, indestructible, and terrible, that pervades his being; that tinges his thoughts; that lurks in his heart; that watches on his lips the struggle of his last breath. In his fear, the mild old Gobila offered extra human sacrifices to all the Evil Spirits that had taken possession of his white friends. His heart was heavy. Some warriors spoke about burning and killing, but the cautious old savage dissuaded them. Who could foresee the woe those mysterious creatures, if irritated, might bring? They should be left alone. Perhaps in time they would disappear into the earth as the first one had disappeared. His people must keep away from them, and hope for the best.

Kayerts and Carlier did not disappear, but remained above on this earth, that, somehow, they fancied had become bigger and very empty. It was not the absolute and dumb solitude of the post that impressed them so much as an inarticulate feeling that something from within them was gone, something that worked for their safety, and had kept the wilderness from interfering with their hearts. The images of home; the memory of people like them, of men that thought and felt as they used to think and feel, receded into distances made indistinct by the glare of unclouded sunshine. And out of the great silence of the surrounding wilderness, its very hopelessness and savagery seemed to approach them nearer, to draw them gently, to look upon them, to envelop them with a solicitude irresistible, familiar, and disgusting.

Days lengthened into weeks, then into months. Gobila's people drummed and yelled to every new moon, as of yore, but kept away from the station. Makola and Carlier tried once in a canoe to open communications, but were received with a shower of arrows, and had to fly back to the station for dear life. That attempt set the country up and down the river into an uproar that could be very distinctly heard for days. The steamer was late. At first they spoke of delay jauntily, then anxiously, then gloomily. The matter was becoming serious. Stores were running short. Carlier cast his lines off the bank, but the river was low, and the fish kept out in the stream. They dared not stroll far away from the station to shoot. Moreover, there was no game in the impenetrable forest. Once Carlier shot a hippo in the river. They had no boat to secure it, and it sank. When it floated up it drifted away, and Gobila's people secured the carcass. It was the occasion for a national holiday, but Carlier had a fit of rage over it and talked about the necessity of exterminating all the negroes before the country could be made habitable. Kayerts mooned about silently; spent hours looking at the portrait of his Melie. It represented a little girl with long bleached tresses and a rather sour face. His legs were much swollen, and he could hardly walk. Carlier, undermined by fever, could not swagger any more, but kept tottering about, still with a devil-may-care air, as became a man who remembered his crack regiment. He had become hoarse, sarcastic, and inclined to say unpleasant things. He called it 'being frank with you'. They had long ago reckoned their percentages on trade, including in them that last deal of 'this infamous Makola'. They had also concluded not to say anything about it. Kayerts hesitated at first—was afraid of the director.

'He has seen worse things done on the quiet,' maintained Carlier, with a hoarse laugh. 'Trust him! He won't thank you if you blab. He is no better than you or me. Who will talk if we hold our tongues? There is nobody here.'

That was the root of the trouble! There was nobody there; and being left there alone with their weakness, they became daily more like a pair of accomplices than like a couple of devoted friends. They had heard nothing from home for eight months. Every evening they said: 'Tomorrow we shall see the steamer.' But one of the

* F

Company's steamers had been wrecked, and the director was busy with the other, relieving very distant and important stations on the main river. He thought that the useless station, and the useless men, could wait. Meantime Kayerts and Carlier lived on rice boiled without salt, and cursed the Company, all Africa, and the day they were born. One must have lived on such diet to discover what ghastly trouble the necessity of swallowing one's food may become. There was literally nothing else in the station but rice and coffee; they drank the coffee without sugar. The last fifteen lumps Kayerts had solemnly locked away in his box, together with a half-bottle of cognac, 'in case of sickness', he explained. Carlier approved. 'When one is sick', he said, 'any little extra like that is cheering.'

They waited. Rank grass began to sprout over the courtyard. The bell never rang now. Days passed, silent, exasperating, and slow. When the two men spoke, they snarled; and their silences were bitter, as if tinged by the bitterness of their thoughts.

One day after a lunch of boiled rice, Carlier put down his cup untasted, and said: 'Hang it all! Let's have a decent cup of coffee for once. Bring out that sugar, Kayerts!'

'For the sick,' muttered Kayerts, without looking up.

'For the sick,' mocked Carlier. 'Bosh! . . . Well! I am sick.'

'You are no more sick than I am, and I go without,' said Kayerts in a peaceful tone.

'Come, out with that sugar, you stingy old slave-dealer.'

Kayerts looked up quickly. Carlier was smiling with marked insolence. And suddenly it seemed to Kayerts that he had never seen that man before. Who was he? He knew nothing about him. What was he capable of? There was a surprising flash of violent emotion within him, as if in the presence of something undreamt-of, dangerous, and final. But he managed to pronounce with composure:

'That joke is in very bad taste. Don't repeat it.'

'Joke!' said Carlier, hitching himself forward on his seat. 'I am hungry—I am sick—I don't joke! I hate hypocrites. You are a hypocrite. You are a slave-dealer. I am a slave-dealer. There's nothing but slave-dealers in this cursed country. I mean to have sugar in my coffee today, anyhow!'

'I forbid you to speak to me in that way,' said Kayerts with a fair show of resolution.

'You! What?' shouted Carlier, jumping up.

Kayerts stood up also. 'I am your chief,' he began, trying to master the shakiness of his voice.

'What?' yelled the other. 'Who's chief? There's no chief here. There's nothing here: there's nothing but you and I. Fetch the sugar—you pot-bellied ass.'

'Hold your tongue! Go out of this room!' screamed Kayerts. 'I dismiss you—you scoundrel!'

Carlier swung a stool. All at once he looked dangerously in earnest. 'You flabby, good-for-nothing civilian—take that!' he howled.

Kayerts dropped under the table, and the stool struck the grass inner wall of the room. Then, as Carlier was trying to upset the table, Kayerts in desperation made a blind rush, head low, like a cornered pig would do, and overturning his friend, bolted along the veranda, and into his room. He locked the door, snatched his revolver, and stood panting. In less than a minute Carlier was kicking at the door furiously, howling: 'If you don't bring out that sugar, I will shoot you at sight, like a dog! Now then—one—two—three! You won't? I will show you who's the master!'

Kayerts thought the door would fall in, and scrambled

through the square hole that served for a window in his room. There was then the whole breadth of the house between them. But the other was apparently not strong enough to break in the door, and Kayerts heard him running round. Then he also began to run laboriously on his swollen legs. He ran as quickly as he could, grasping the revolver, and unable yet to understand what was happening to him. He saw in succession Makola's house, the store, the river, the ravine, and the low bushes; and he saw all those things again as he ran for the second time round the house. Then again they flashed past him. That morning he could not have walked a yard without a groan.

And now he ran. He ran fast enough to keep out of sight of the other man.

Then as, weak and desperate, he thought, 'Before I finish the next round I shall die,' he heard the other man stumble heavily, then stop. He stopped also. He had the back and Carlier the front of the house, as before. He heard him drop into a chair cursing, and suddenly his own legs gave way, and he slid down into a sitting posture with his back to the wall. His mouth was as dry as a cinder, and his face was wet with perspiration—and tears. What was it all about? He thought it must be a horrible illusion; he thought he was dreaming; he thought he was going mad! After a while he collected his senses. What did they quarrel about? That sugar! How absurd! He would give it to him—didn't want it himself. And he began scrambling to his feet with a sudden feeling of security. But before he had fairly stood upright, a common-sense reflection occurred to him and drove him back into despair. He thought: 'If I give way now to that brute of a soldier, he will begin this horror again tomorrow—and the day after—every day—raise other pretensions, trample on me, torture me, make me his slave—and I will be lost! Lost! The steamer may not come for days—may never come.' He shook so that he had to sit down on the floor again. He shivered forlornly. He felt he could not, would not, move any more. He was completely distracted by the sudden perception that the position was without issue—that death and life had in a moment become equally difficult and terrible.

All at once he heard the other push his chair back; and he leaped to his feet with extreme facility. He listened and got confused. Must run again! Right or left? He heard footsteps. He darted to the left, grasping his revolver, and at the very same instant, as it seemed to him, they came into violent collision. Both shouted with surprise. A loud explosion took place between them; a roar of red fire, thick smoke; and Kayerts, deafened and blinded, rushed back thinking: 'I am hit—it's all over.' He expected the other to come round—to gloat over his agony. He caught hold of an upright of the roof. 'All over!' Then he heard a crashing fall on the other side of the house, as if somebody had tumbled headlong over a chair—then silence. Nothing more happened. He did not die. Only his shoulder felt as if it had been badly wrenched, and he had lost his revolver. He was disarmed and helpless! He waited for his fate. The other man made no sound. It was a stratagem. He was stalking him now! Along what side? Perhaps he was taking aim this very minute!

After a few moments of an agony frightful and absurd, he decided to go and meet his doom. He was prepared for every surrender. He turned the corner, steadying himself with one hand on the wall; made a few paces, and nearly swooned. He had seen on the floor, protruding past the other corner, a pair of turned-up feet. A pair of white naked feet in red slippers. He felt deadly sick, and stood for a time in profound darkness. Then Makola appeared before him, saying quietly: 'Come along, Mr Kayerts. He is dead.' He burst into tears of gratitude; a loud, sobbing fit of crying. After a time he found himself sitting in a chair and looking at Carlier, who lay stretched on his back. Makola was kneeling over the body.

'Is this your revolver?' asked Makola, getting up.

'Yes,' said Kayerts; then he added very quickly: 'He ran after me to shoot me—you saw!'

'Yes, I saw,' said Makola. 'There is only one revolver; where's his?'

'Don't know,' whispered Kayerts in a voice that had become suddenly very faint.

'I will go and look for it,' said the other gently. He made the round along the veranda, while Kayerts sat still and looked at the corpse. Makola came back empty-handed, stood in deep thought, then stepped quietly into the dead man's room, and came out directly with a revolver, which he held up before Kayerts. Kayerts shut his eyes. Everything was going round. He found life more terrible and difficult than death. He had shot an unarmed man.

After meditating for a while, Makola said softly, pointing at the dead man who lay there with his right eye blown out: 'He died of fever.' Kayerts looked at him with a stony stare. 'Yes,' repeated Makola, thoughtfully, stepping over the corpse, 'I think he died of fever. Bury him tomorrow.'

And he went away slowly to his expectant wife, leaving the two white men alone on the veranda.

Night came, and Kayerts sat unmoving on his chair. He sat quiet as if he had taken a dose of opium. The violence of the emotions he had passed through produced a feeling of exhausted serenity. He had plumbed in one short afternoon the depths of horror and despair, and now found repose in the conviction that life had no more secrets for him: neither had death! He sat by the corpse thinking; thinking very actively, thinking very new thoughts. He seemed to have broken loose from himself altogether. His old thoughts, convictions, likes and dislikes, things he respected and things he abhorred, appeared in their true light at last! Appeared contemptible and childish, false and ridiculous. He revelled in his new wisdom while he sat by the man he had killed. He argued with himself about all things under heaven with that kind of wrong-headed lucidity which may be observed in some lunatics. Incidentally he reflected that the fellow dead there had been a noxious beast anyway; that men died every day in thousands; perhaps in hundreds of thousands —who could tell?—and that in the number, that one death could not possibly make any difference; couldn't have any importance, at least to a thinking creature. He, Kayerts, was a thinking creature. He had been all his life, till that moment, a believer in a lot of nonsense like the rest of mankind—who are fools; but now he thought! He knew! He was at peace; he was familiar with the highest wisdom! Then he tried to imagine himself dead, and Carlier sitting in his chair watching him; and his attempt met with such unexpected success, that in a very few moments he became not at all sure who was dead and who was alive. This extraordinary achievement of his fancy startled him, however, and by a clever and timely effort of mind he saved himself just in time from becoming Carlier. His heart thumped, and he felt hot all over at the thought of that danger. Carlier! What a beastly thing! To compose his now disturbed nerves—and no wonder!—he tried to whistle a little. Then, suddenly, he fell asleep, or thought he had slept; but at any rate there was a fog, and somebody had whistled in the fog.

He stood up. The day had come, and a heavy mist had descended upon the land: the mist penetrating, enveloping, and silent; the morning mist of tropical lands; the mist that clings and kills; the mist white and deadly, immaculate and poisonous. He stood up, saw the body, and threw his arms above his head with a cry like that of a man who, waking from a trance, finds himself immured for ever in a tomb. '*Help!* . . . *My God!*'

A shriek inhuman, vibrating and sudden, pierced like a sharp dart the white shroud of that land of sorrow. Three short, impatient screeches followed, and then, for a time, the fog wreaths rolled on, undisturbed, through a formidable silence. Then many more shrieks, rapid and piercing, like the yells of some exasperated and ruthless creature, rent the air. Progress was calling to Kayerts from the river. Progress and civilization and all the virtues. Society was calling to its accomplished child to come, to be taken care of, to be instructed, to be judged, to be condemned; it called him to return to that rubbish heap from which he had wandered away, so that justice could be done.

Kayerts heard and understood. He stumbled out of the veranda, leaving the other man quite alone for the first time since they had been thrown there together. He groped his way through the fog, calling in his ignorance upon the invisible heaven to undo its work. Makola flitted by in the mist, shouting as he ran:

'Steamer! Steamer! They can't see. They whistle for the station. I go ring the bell. Go down to the landing, sir. I ring.'

He disappeared. Kayerts stood still. He looked upwards; the fog rolled low over his head. He looked round like a man who has lost his way; and he saw a dark smudge, a cross-shaped stain, upon the shifting purity of the mist. As he began to stumble towards it, the station bell rang in a tumultuous peal its answer to the impatient clamour of the steamer.

The Managing Director of the Great Civilizing Company

(since we know that civilization follows trade) landed first, and incontinently lost sight of the steamer. The fog down by the river was exceedingly dense; above, at the station, the bell rang unceasing and brazen.

The director shouted loudly to the steamer:

'There is nobody down to meet us; there may be something wrong, though they are ringing. You had better come, too!'

And he began to toil up the steep bank. The captain and the engine-driver of the boat followed behind. As they scrambled up the fog thinned, and they could see their director a good way ahead. Suddenly they saw him start forward, calling to them over his shoulder: 'Run! Run to the house! I've found one of them! Run, look for the other!'

He had found one of them! And even he, the man of varied and startling experience, was somewhat discomposed by the manner of this finding. He stood and fumbled in his pockets (for a knife) while he faced Kayerts, who was hanging by a leather strap from the cross. He had evidently climbed the grave, which was high and narrow, and after tying the end of the strap to the arm, had swung himself off. His toes were only a couple of inches above the ground; his arms hung stiffly down; he seemed to be standing rigidly at attention, but with one purple cheek playfully posed on the shoulder. And, irreverently, he was putting out a swollen tongue at his Managing Director.

THE LAGOON

THE LAGOON

THE white man, leaning with both arms over the roof of the little house in the stern of the boat, said to the steersman:

'We will pass the night in Arsat's clearing. It is late.'

The Malay only grunted, and went on looking fixedly at the river. The white man rested his chin on his crossed arms and gazed at the wake of the boat. At the end of the straight avenue of forests cut by the intense glitter of the river, the sun appeared unclouded and dazzling, poised low over the water that shone smoothly like a band of metal. The forests, sombre and dull, stood motionless and silent on each side of the broad stream. At the foot of big, towering trees, trunkless nipa palms rose from the mud of the bank, in bunches of leaves enormous and heavy, that hung unstirring over the brown swirl of eddies. In the stillness of the air every tree, every leaf, every bough, every tendril of creeper, and every petal of minute blossoms seemed to have been bewitched into an immobility perfect and final. Nothing moved on the river but the eight paddles that rose flashing regularly, dipped together with a single splash; while the steersman swept right and left with a periodic and sudden flourish of his blade describing a glinting semicircle above his head. The churned-up water frothed alongside with a confused murmur. And the white man's canoe, advancing upstream in the short-lived disturbance of its own making, seemed to enter the portals of a land from which the very memory of motion had for ever departed.

The white man, turning his back upon the setting sun, looked along the empty and broad expanse of the sea reach. For the last three miles of its course the wandering, hesitating river, as if enticed irresistibly by the freedom of an open horizon, flows straight into the sea, flows straight to the east—to the east that harbours both light and darkness. Astern of the boat the repeated call of some bird, a cry discordant and feeble, skipped along over the smooth water and lost itself, before it could reach the other shore, in the breathless silence of the world.

The steersman dug his paddle into the stream, and held hard with stiffened arms, his body thrown forward. The water gurgled aloud; and suddenly the long straight reach seemed to pivot on its centre, the forests swung in a semicircle, and the slanting beams of sunset touched the broadside of the canoe with a fiery glow, throwing the slender and distorted shadows of its crew upon the streaked glitter of the river. The white man turned to look ahead. The course of the boat had been altered at right-angles to the stream, and the carved dragon-head of its prow was pointing now at a gap in the fringing bushes of the bank. It glided through, brushing the overhanging twigs, and disappeared from the river like some slim and amphibious creature leaving the water for its lair in the forests.

The narrow creek was like a ditch: tortuous, fabulously deep; filled with gloom under the thin strip of pure and shining blue of the heaven. Immense trees soared up, invisible behind the festooned draperies of creepers. Here and there, near the glistening blackness of the water, a twisted root of some tall tree showed amongst the tracery of small ferns, black and dull, writhing and motionless, like an arrested snake. The short words of the paddlers reverberated loudly between the thick and sombre walls of vegetation. Darkness oozed out from between the trees, through the tangled maze of the creepers, from behind the great fantastic and unstirring leaves; the darkness, mysterious and invincible; the darkness scented and poisonous of impenetrable forests.

The men poled in the shoaling water. The creek broadened, opening out into a wide sweep of a stagnant lagoon. The forests receded from the marshy bank, leaving a level strip of bright green, reedy grass to frame the reflected blueness of the sky. A fleecy pink cloud drifted high above, trailing the delicate colouring of its image under the floating leaves and the silvery blossoms of the lotus. A little house, perched on high piles, appeared black in the distance. Near it two tall nibong palms, that seemed to have come out of the forests in the background, leaned slightly over the ragged roof, with a suggestion of sad tenderness and care in the droop of their leafy and soaring heads.

The steersman, pointing with his paddle, said: 'Arsat is there. I see his canoe fast between the piles.'

The polers ran along the sides of the boat glancing over their shoulders at the end of the day's journey. They would have preferred to spend the night somewhere else than on this lagoon of weird aspect and ghostly reputation. Moreover, they disliked Arsat, first as a stranger, and also because he who repairs a ruined house, and dwells in it, proclaims that he is not afraid to live amongst the spirits that haunt the places abandoned by mankind. Such a man can disturb the course of fate by glances or words; while his familiar ghosts are not easy to propitiate by casual wayfarers upon whom they long to wreak the malice of their human master. White men care not for such things, being unbelievers and in league with the Father of

Evil, who leads them unharmed through the invisible dangers of this world. To the warnings of the righteous they oppose an offensive pretence of disbelief. What is there to be done?

So they thought, throwing their weight on the end of their long poles. The big canoe glided on swiftly, noiselessly, and smoothly, towards Arsat's clearing, till, in a great rattling of poles thrown down, and the loud murmurs of 'Allah be praised!' it came with a gentle knock against the crooked piles below the house.

The boatmen with uplifted faces shouted discordantly: 'Arsat! O Arsat!' Nobody came. The white man began to climb the rude ladder giving access to the bamboo platform before the house. The juragan of the boat said sulkily: 'We will cook in the sampan, and sleep on the water.'

'Pass my blankets and the basket,' said the white man, curtly.

He knelt on the edge of the platform to receive the bundle. Then the boat shoved off, and the white man, standing up, confronted Arsat, who had come out through the low door of his hut. He was a man young, powerful, with broad chest and muscular arms. He had nothing on but his sarong. His head was bare. His big, soft eyes stared eagerly at the white man, but his voice and demeanour were composed as he asked, without any words of greeting:

'Have you medicine, Tuan?'

'No,' said the visitor in a startled tone. 'No. Why? Is there sickness in the house?'

'Enter and see,' replied Arsat, in the same calm manner, and turning short round, passed again through the small doorway. The white man, dropping his bundles, followed.

In the dim light of the dwelling he made out on a couch of bamboos a woman stretched on her back under a broad sheet of red cotton cloth. She lay still, as if dead;

but her big eyes, wide open, glittered in the gloom, staring upwards at the slender rafters, motionless and unseeing. She was in a high fever, and evidently unconscious. Her cheeks were sunk slightly, her lips were partly open, and on the young face there was the ominous and fixed expression—the absorbed, contemplating expression of the unconscious who are going to die. The two men stood looking down at her in silence.

'Has she been long ill?' asked the traveller.

'I have not slept for five nights,' answered the Malay, in a deliberate tone. 'At first she heard voices calling her from the water and struggled against me who held her. But since the sun of today rose she hears nothing—she hears not me. She sees nothing. She sees not me—me!' He remained silent for a minute, then asked softly: 'Tuan, will she die?'

'I fear so,' said the white man, sorrowfully. He had known Arsat years ago, in a far country in times of trouble and danger, when no friendship is to be despised. And since his Malay friend had come unexpectedly to dwell in the hut on the lagoon with a strange woman, he had slept many times there, in his journeys up and down the river. He liked the man who knew how to keep faith in council and how to fight without fear by the side of his white friend. He liked him—not so much perhaps as a man likes his favourite dog, but still he liked him well enough to help and ask no questions, to think sometimes vaguely and hazily in the midst of his own pursuits, about the lonely man and the long-haired woman with audacious face and triumphant eyes, who lived together hidden by the forests—alone and feared.

The white man came out of the hut in time to see the enormous conflagration of sunset put out by the swift and stealthy shadows that, rising like a black and impalpable vapour above the tree tops, spread over the heaven, extinguishing the crimson glow of floating clouds and the red brilliance of departing daylight. In a few moments all the stars came out above the intense blackness of the earth, and the great lagoon gleaming suddenly with reflected lights resembled an oval patch of night sky flung down into the hopeless and abysmal night of the wilderness. The white man had some supper out of the basket, then collecting a few sticks that lay about the platform, made up a small fire, not for warmth, but for the sake of the smoke, which would keep off the mosquitoes. He wrapped himself in the blankets and sat with his back against the reed wall of the house, smoking thoughtfully.

Arsat came through the doorway with noiseless steps and squatted down by the fire. The white man moved his outstretched legs a little.

'She breathes,' said Arsat in a low voice, anticipating the expected question. 'She breathes and burns as if with a great fire. She speaks not; she hears not—and burns!' He paused for a moment, then asked in a quiet, incurious tone: 'Tuan . . . will she die?'

The white man moved his shoulders uneasily and muttered in a hesitating manner:

'If such is her fate.'

'No, Tuan,' said Arsat, calmly. 'If such is my fate. I hear, I see, I wait. I remember . . . Tuan, do you remember the old days? Do you remember my brother?'

'Yes,' said the white man. The Malay rose suddenly and went in. The other, sitting still outside, could hear the voice in the hut. Arsat said: 'Hear me! Speak!' His words were succeeded by a complete silence. 'O Diamelen!' he cried, suddenly. After that cry there was a deep sigh. Arsat came out and sank down again in his old place.

They sat in silence before the fire. There was no sound within the house, there was no sound near them; but far

away on the lagoon they could hear the voices of the
boatmen ringing fitful and distinct on the calm water.
The fire in the bows of the sampan shone faintly in the
distance with a hazy red glow. Then it died out. The
voices ceased. The land and the water slept invisible,
unstirring and mute. It was as though there had been
nothing left in the world but the glitter of stars stream-
ing, ceaseless and vain, through the black stillness of
the night.

The white man gazed straight before him into the
darkness with wide-open eyes. The fear and fascination,
the inspiration and the wonder of death—of death near,
unavoidable, and unseen, soothed the unrest of his race
and stirred the most indistinct, the most intimate of his
thoughts. The ever-ready suspicion of evil, the gnawing
suspicion that lurks in our hearts, flowed out into the
stillness round him—into the stillness profound and dumb,
and made it appear untrustworthy and infamous, like the
placid and impenetrable mask of an unjustifiable violence.
In that fleeting and powerful disturbance of his being the
earth enfolded in the starlight peace became a shadowy
country of inhuman strife, a battlefield of phantoms
terrible and charming, august or ignoble, struggling
ardently for the possession of our helpless hearts. An
unquiet and mysterious country of inextinguishable
desires and fears.

A plaintive murmur rose in the night; a murmur
saddening and startling, as if the great solitudes of
surrounding woods had tried to whisper into his ear the
wisdom of their immense and lofty indifference. Sounds
hesitating and vague floated in the air round him, shaped
themselves slowly into words; and at last flowed on gently
in a murmuring stream of soft and monotonous sentences.
He stirred like a man waking up and changed his position
slightly. Arsat, motionless and shadowy, sitting with

bowed head under the stars, was speaking in a low and dreamy tone:

'. . . for where can we lay down the heaviness of our trouble but in a friend's heart? A man must speak of war and of love. You, Tuan, know what war is, and you have seen me in time of danger seek death as other men seek life! A writing may be lost; a lie may be written; but what the eye has seen is truth and remains in the mind!'

'I remember,' said the white man, quietly.

Arsat went on with mournful composure:

'Therefore I shall speak to you of love. Speak in the night. Speak before both night and love are gone—and the eye of day looks upon my sorrow and my shame; upon my blackened face; upon my burnt-up heart.'

A sigh, short and faint, marked an almost imperceptible pause, and then his words flowed on, without a stir, without a gesture.

'After the time of trouble and war was over and you went away from my country in the pursuit of your desires, which we, men of the islands, cannot understand, I and my brother became again, as we had been before, the sword-bearers of the Ruler. You know we were men of family, belonging to a ruling race, and more fit than any to carry on our right shoulder the emblem of power. And in the time of prosperity Si Dendring showed us favour, as we, in time of sorrow, had showed to him the faithfulness of our courage. It was a time of peace. A time of deer hunts and cock fights; of idle talks and foolish squabbles between men whose bellies are full and weapons are rusty. But the sower watched the young rice shoots grow up without fear, and the traders came and went, departed lean and returned fat into the river of peace. They brought news, too. Brought lies and truth mixed together, so that no man knew when to rejoice and when to be sorry. We heard from them about you also. They had seen you here and had seen you there. And I was glad to hear, for I remembered the stirring times, and I always remembered you, Tuan, till the time came when my eyes could see nothing in the past, because they had looked upon the one who is dying there—in the house.'

He stopped to exclaim in an intense whisper, 'O Mara bahia! O calamity!' then went on speaking a little louder:

'There's no worse enemy and no better friend than a brother, Tuan, for one brother knows another, and in perfect knowledge is strength for good or evil. I loved my brother. I went to him and told him that I could see nothing but one face, hear nothing but one voice. He told me: "Open your heart so that she can see what is in it—and wait. Patience is wisdom. Inchi Midah may die or our Ruler may throw off his fear of a woman!" . . . I waited! . . . You remember the lady with the veiled face, Tuan, and the fear of our Ruler before her cunning and temper. And if she wanted her servant, what could I do? But I fed the hunger of my heart on short glances and stealthy words. I loitered on the path to the bath-houses in the daytime, and when the sun had fallen behind the forest I crept along the jasmine hedges of the women's courtyard. Unseeing, we spoke to one another through the scent of flowers, through the veil of leaves, through the blades of long grass that stood still before our lips; so great was our prudence, so faint was the murmur of our great longing. The time passed swiftly . . . and there were whispers amongst women—and our enemies watched— my brother was gloomy, and I began to think of killing and of a fierce death. . . . We are of a people who take what they want—like you whites. There is a time when a man should forget loyalty and respect. Might and authority are given to rulers, but to all men is given love and strength and courage. My brother said: "You shall take her from their midst. We are two who are like one."

And I answered: "Let it be soon, for I find no warmth in sunlight that does not shine upon her." Our time came when the Ruler and all the great people went to the mouth of the river to fish by torchlight. There were hundreds of boats, and on the white sand, between the water and the forests, dwellings of leaves were built for the households of the Rajahs. The smoke of cooking-fires was like a blue mist of the evening, and many voices rang in it joyfully. While they were making the boats ready to beat up the fish, my brother came to me and said, "Tonight!" I looked to my weapons, and when the time came our canoe took its place in the circle of boats carrying the torches. The lights blazed on the water, but behind the boats there was darkness. When the shouting began and the excitement made them like mad we dropped out. The water swallowed our fire, and we floated back to the shore that was dark with only here and there the glimmer of embers. We could hear the talk of slave girls amongst the sheds. Then we found a place deserted and silent. We waited there. She came. She came running along the shore, rapid and leaving no trace, like a leaf driven by the wind into the sea. My brother said gloomily: "Go and take her; carry her into our boat." I lifted her in my arms. She panted. Her heart was beating against my breast. I said: "I take you from those people. You came to the cry of my heart, but my arms take you into my boat against the will of the great!" "It is right," said my brother. "We are men who take what we want and can hold it against many. We should have taken her in daylight." I said, "Let us be off"; for since she was in my boat I began to think of our Ruler's many men. "Yes. Let us be off," said my brother. "We are cast out and this boat is our country now—and the sea is our refuge." He lingered with his foot on the shore, and I entreated him to hasten, for I remembered the strokes of her heart against my breast and thought that two men cannot withstand a hundred. We left, paddllng downstream close to the bank; and as we passed by the creek where they were fishing, the great shouting had ceased, but the murmur of voices was loud like the humming of insects flying at noonday. The boats floated, clustered together, in the red light of torches, under a black roof of smoke; and men talked of their sport. Men that boasted and praised and jeered—men that would have been our friends in the morning, but on that night were already our enemies. We paddled swiftly past. We had no more friends in the country of our birth. She sat in the middle of the canoe with covered face; silent as she is now; unseeing as she is now—and I had no regret at what I was leaving because I could hear her breathing close to me—as I can hear her now.'

He paused, listened with his ear turned to the doorway, then shook his head and went on:

'My brother wanted to shout the cry of challenge—one cry only—to let the people know we were freeborn robbers who trusted our arms and the great sea. And again I begged him in the name of our love to be silent. Could I not hear her breathing close to me? I knew the pursuit would come quick enough. My brother loved me. He dipped his paddle without a splash. He only said: "There is half a man in you now—the other half is in that woman. I can wait. When you are a whole man again, you will come back with me here to shout defiance. We are sons of the same mother." I made no answer. All my strength and all my spirit were in my hands that held the paddle—for I longed to be with her in a safe place beyond the reach of men's anger and of women's spite. My love was so great, that I thought it could guide me to a country where death was unknown, if I could only escape from Inchi Midah's fury and from our Ruler's sword. We paddled with haste, breathing through our teeth. The blades bit deep into the smooth water. We passed out of the river; we flew in clear channels amongst the shallows. We skirted the black coast; we skirted the sand beaches where the sea speaks in whispers to the land; and the gleam of white sand flashed back past our boat, so swiftly she ran upon the water. We spoke not. Only once I said: "Sleep, Diamelen, for soon you may want all your strength." I heard the sweetness of her voice, but I never turned my head. The sun rose and still we went on. Water fell from my face like rain from a cloud. We flew in the light and heat. I never looked back, but I knew that my brother's eyes, behind me, were looking steadily ahead, for the boat went as straight as a bushman's dart, when it leaves the end of the sumpitan. There was no better paddler, no better steersman than my brother. Many times, together, we had won races in that canoe. But we never had put out our strength as we did then—then, when for the last time we paddled together! There was no braver or stronger man in our country than my brother. I could not spare the strength to turn my head and look at him, but every moment I heard the hiss of his breath getting louder behind me. Still he did not speak. The sun was high. The heat clung to my back like a flame of fire. My ribs were ready to burst, but I could no longer get enough air into my chest. And then I felt I must cry out with my last breath: "Let us rest!" . . . "Good!" he answered; and his voice was firm. He was strong. He was brave. He knew not fear and no fatigue . . . My brother!'

A murmur powerful and gentle, a murmur vast and faint; the murmur of trembling leaves, of stirring boughs, ran through the tangled depths of the forests, ran over the starry smoothness of the lagoon, and the water between the piles lapped the slimy timber once with a sudden splash. A breath of warm air touched the two men's faces and passed on with a mournful sound—a breath loud and short like an uneasy sigh of the dreaming earth.

Arsat went on in an even, low voice.

'We ran our canoe on the white beach of a little bay close to a long tongue of land that seemed to bar our road; a long wooded cape going far into the sea. My brother knew that place. Beyond the cape a river has its entrance, and through the jungle of that land there is a narrow path. We made a fire and cooked rice. Then we lay down to sleep on the soft sand in the shade of our canoe, while she watched. No sooner had I closed my eyes than I heard her cry of alarm. We leaped up. The sun was half way down the sky already, and coming in sight in the opening of the bay we saw a prau manned by many paddlers. We knew it at once; it was one of our Rajah's praus. They were watching the shore, and saw us. They beat the gong, and turned the head of the prau into the bay. I felt my heart become weak within my breast. Diamelen sat on the sand and covered her face. There was no escape by sea. My brother laughed. He had the gun you had given him, Tuan, before you went away, but there was only a handful of powder. He spoke to me quickly: "Run with her along the path. I shall keep them back, for they have no firearms, and landing in the face of a man with a gun is certain death for some. Run with her. On the other side of that wood there is a fisherman's house—and a canoe. When I have fired all the shots I will follow. I am a great runner, and before they can come up we shall be gone. I will hold out as long as I can, for she is but a woman—that can neither run nor fight, but she has your heart in her weak hands." He dropped behind the canoe. The prau was coming. She and I ran, and as we rushed along the path I heard shots. My brother fired—once—twice—and the booming of the gong ceased. There was silence behind us. That neck of land is narrow. Before I heard my brother fire the third shot I saw the shelving shore, and I saw the water again; the mouth of a broad river. We crossed a grassy glade. We ran down to the water. I saw a low hut above the black mud, and a small canoe hauled up. I heard another shot behind me. I thought: "That is his last charge." We rushed down to the canoe; a man came running from the hut, but I leaped on him, and we rolled together in the mud. Then I got up, and he lay still at my feet. I don't know whether I had killed him or not. I and Diamelen pushed the canoe afloat. I heard yells behind me, and I saw my brother run across the glade. Many men were bounding after him, I took her in my arms and threw her into the boat, then leaped in myself. When I looked back I saw that my brother had fallen. He fell and was up again, but the men were closing round him. He shouted: "I am coming!" The men were close to him. I looked. Many men. Then I looked at her. Tuan, I pushed the canoe! I pushed it into deep water. She was kneeling forward looking at me, and I said, "Take your paddle", while I struck the water with mine. Tuan, I heard him cry. I heard him cry my name twice; and I heard voices shouting: "Kill! Strike!" I never turned back. I heard him calling my name again with a great shriek, as when life is going out together with the voice—and I never turned my head. My own name! . . . My brother! Three times he called—but I was not afraid of life. Was she not there in that canoe? And could I not with her find a country where death is forgotten—where death is unknown!'

The white man sat up. Arsat rose and stood, an indistinct and silent figure above the dying embers of the fire. Over the lagoon a mist drifting and low had crept, erasing slowly the glittering images of the stars. And now a great expanse of white vapour covered the land: it flowed cold and grey in the darkness, eddied in noiseless whirls round the tree trunks and about the platform of the house, which seemed to float upon a restless and impalpable illusion of a sea. Only far away the tops of the trees stood outlined on the twinkle of heaven, like a sombre and forbidding shore—a coast deceptive, pitiless and black.

Arsat's voice vibrated loudly in the profound peace.

'I had her there! I had her! To get her I would have faced all mankind. But I had her—and——'

His words went out ringing into the empty distances. He paused, and seemed to listen to them dying away very far—beyond help and beyond recall. Then he said quietly:

'Tuan, I loved my brother.'

A breath of wind made him shiver. High above his head, high above the silent sea of mist the drooping leaves of the palms rattled together with a mournful and expiring sound. The white man stretched his legs. His chin rested on his chest, and he murmured sadly without lifting his head:

'We all love our brothers.'

Arsat burst out with an intense whispering violence:

'What did I care who died? I wanted peace in my own heart.'

He seemed to hear a stir in the house—listened—then stepped in noiselessly. The white man stood up. A breeze was coming in fitful puffs. The stars shone paler as if they had retreated into the frozen depths of immense space. After a chill gust of wind there were a few seconds of perfect calm and absolute silence. Then from behind the black and wavy line of the forests a column of golden light shot up into the heavens and spread over the semicircle of the eastern horizon. The sun had risen. The mist lifted, broke into drifting patches, vanished into thin flying wreaths; and the unveiled lagoon lay, polished and black, in the heavy shadows at the foot of the wall of trees. A white eagle rose over it with a slanting and ponderous flight, reached the clear sunshine and appeared dazzlingly brilliant for a moment, then soaring higher, became a dark and motionless speck before it vanished into the blue as if it had left the earth for ever. The white man, standing gazing upwards before the doorway, heard in the hut a confused and broken murmur of distracted words ending with a loud groan. Suddenly Arsat stumbled out with outstretched hands, shivered, and stood still for some time with fixed eyes. Then he said:

'She burns no more.'

Before his face the sun showed its edge above the tree tops rising steadily. The breeze freshened; a great brilliance burst upon the lagoon, sparkled on the rippling water. The forests came out of the clear shadows of the morning, became distinct, as if they had rushed nearer—to stop short in a great stir of leaves, of nodding boughs, of swaying branches. In the merciless sunshine the whisper of unconscious life grew louder, speaking in an incomprehensible voice round the dumb darkness of that human sorrow. Arsat's eyes wandered slowly, then stared at the rising sun.

'I can see nothing,' he said half aloud to himself.

'There is nothing,' said the white man, moving to the edge of the platform and waving his hand to his boat. A shout came faintly over the lagoon and the sampan began to glide towards the abode of the friend of ghosts.

'If you want to come with me, I will wait all the morning,' said the white man, looking away upon the water.

'No, Tuan,' said Arsat, softly. 'I shall not eat or sleep in this house, but I must first see my road. Now I can see nothing—see nothing! There is no light and no peace in the world; but there is death—death for many. We are sons of the same mother—and I left him in the midst of enemies; but I am going back now.' He drew a long breath and went on in a dreamy tone: 'In a little while I shall see clear enough to strike—to strike. But she has died, and . . . now . . . darkness.'

He flung his arms wide open, let them fall along his body, then stood still with unmoved face and stony eyes, staring at the sun. The white man got down into his canoe. The polers ran smartly along the sides of the boat, looking over their shoulders at the beginning of a weary journey. High in the stern, his head muffled up in white rags, the juragan sat moody, letting his paddle trail in the water. The white man, leaning with both arms over the grass roof of the little cabin, looked back at the shining ripple of the boat's wake. Before the sampan passed out of the lagoon into the creek he lifted his eyes. Arsat had not moved. He stood lonely in the searching sunshine; and he looked beyond the great light of a cloudless day into the darkness of a world of illusions.

NOTES TO HEART OF DARKNESS

(The biographical notes have been compiled from
several sources, but most particularly from the 'Congo
Diary', and G. Jean-Aubry's books *The Sea Dreamer :
Joseph Conrad* and *Joseph Conrad in the Congo*. Jean-
Aubry develops many more parallels between the
novel and Conrad's own experience than are indicated
here, but the intention is to give an adequate rather
than a complete picture of the relationship between
fact and fiction in the novel.)

p. 3   1. The flood had made—the tide was coming in ('flood'
        is the opposite of 'ebb').

p. 3   2. Gravesend—a district of London. The sound of the
        name is ominous here.

p. 3   3. Already said somewhere—see the opening paragraph
        of Conrad's novel *Youth*.

p. 5   4. The first narrator sees British imperial exploration
        as the 'tale' of a holy quest, of a noble service to
        mankind such as the medieval knights dedicated
        themselves to. Sir Francis Drake (1541–1596),
        Elizabeth I's great captain, established England's
        supremacy over Spain on the high seas by defeating
        the Spanish Armada and raiding Spanish possessions.
        He was also an explorer, the first Englishman to
        circumnavigate the globe. His ship was the *Golden
        Hind*. Drake is regarded as the embodiment of the
        English naval tradition of fearless enterprise.

Sir John Franklin (1786–1847) was an explorer from another period of empire-building. He commanded two expeditions to the North American shores of the Arctic Ocean, and a later one to discover the North West Passage. The two ships of the later expedition were the *Erebus* and *Terror* (the name Erebus is taken from Greek mythology and signifies the infernal regions through which souls passed to Hades). Franklin can be credited with the discovery of the North West Passage, though the ships were caught in the ice and abandoned, and Franklin and his crew died on the overland trek forced upon them.

p. 5 5. Deptford, Greenwich, and Erith are all places on the Thames in London close to where the *Nellie* is.

p. 5 6. 'on 'Change' is an abbreviation of 'on the Exchange', i.e. a place where merchants meet for commercial transactions. The first narrator is thinking of the distinctions between ships of England's Navy and private merchant ships.

p. 5 7. Queen Elizabeth incorporated England's East India Company by royal charter on December 31st, 1600. It largely confined its efforts to India, where it not only enjoyed a monopoly on trade but also became the British government's administration, its members having great influence in Parliament. The great profits it enjoyed in the seventeenth century had encouraged private traders to challenge the royal monopoly granted the Company. These traders were called 'interlopers', and their challenge to the commissioned 'generals' of the Company led to a new Act in 1698 which founded a new East India Company. In the nineteenth century the Company ceased to be a trading concern and exercised an administrative function until the Indian Mutiny (1857) forced the transference of administration to the Crown in 1858.

p. 7   8. trireme—an ancient galley (originally Greek, afterwards also Roman) with three ranks of oars one above
another, used chiefly as a ship of war.

p. 7   9. Falernian wine—a famous wine from the rich, level
district of Campagna di Roma, Italy, which lies
southeast of the Tiber.

p. 7   10. Ravenna—a town of the region Cisalpine Gaul, which
lay south of the Alps. The emperor Augustus made it
one of the two chief stations of the Roman fleet.

p. 8   11. Buddha—a deified infallible religious teacher of the
Buddhists. The term is especially applied to Gautama
Siddhartha, founder of an order of wandering monks
who taught what is now called Early Buddhism.
'Buddha' in Sanskrit means 'awakened, enlightened'.
Buddhism teaches that nirvana, release from liability
to suffering, from mortality, is the highest goal attain-
able now or hereafter. The eight petals of the Indian
lotus symbolize the 'noble eightfold path' taught by
Gautama Buddha, and the spread of Buddhism
carried the lotus design throughout the Orient. The
lotus thrones of the Buddhist gods rise above the
impure earth, just as the Indian lotus holds its head
above the water. (See question 10 of Exploring the
Structure.)

pp. 9–10 12. In *A Personal Record* Conrad wrote:
It was in 1868, when nine years old or thereabouts,
that while looking at a map of Africa of the time
and putting my finger on the blank space then
representing the unsolved mystery of that continent,
I said to myself with absolute assurance and an
amazing audacity which are no longer in my
character now: 'When I grow up I shall go *there*.'
And of course I thought no more about it till
after a quarter of a century or so an opportunity
offered to go there—as if the sin of childish audacity
was to be visited on my mature head.

*G

p. 10   13. The Company Conrad applied to was the Société Anonyme Belge pour le Commerce du Haut-Congo.

p. 10   14. Fleet Street—a well-known London street; the heart of the newspaper industry.

p. 11   15. Marlow is giving an exact account of Conrad's experience here. His aunt in Brussels was Madame Marguerite Poradowska, a woman with literary aspirations. It was largely through her efforts and efforts of influential friends that Conrad was given the appointment.

p. 11   16. The name of the actual captain killed was Freiesleben. He was a Dane. Most of the captains and engineers on the Congo at the time were Scandinavian.

p. 12   17. A letter from Conrad to his cousin states that he did have only three days in which to prepare for three years in the middle of Africa.

p. 12   18. The 'whited sepulchre' is Brussels.

p. 14   19. *Ave*—Farewell.
Morituri te salutant—They who are about to die salute thee. This salutation seems to be a variation of the well-known cry of the Roman gladiators to the emperor, 'Morituri te salutamus', which means, 'We who are about to die salute thee.'

p. 15   20. alienist—one who treats or makes a specialty of things of the mind. A psychiatrist.

p. 17   21. Conrad sailed on the *Ville de Maceio* to Boma, which was the administration centre of the independent state of the Congo. The details described are no doubt authentic, since France was beginning to campaign in these parts. Conrad went as a passenger from Boma to Matadi, the Company's station. His work was scheduled to start at Stanley Pool, some 200 miles farther up river. (See endpaper map.)

pp. 20–1 22. The railroad between Matadi and Kinchassa had just been started.

Yale University Photographic Services

MATADI IN 1893

p. 24   23. There is no record of the accountant.

pp. 25–6   24. Mr Kurtz is probably drawn from a Mr Georges Antoine Klein, an agent of the Company, who, the records show, died on board the steamer *Roi des Belges* from the effects of dysentery.

p. 28   25. The unhealthy companion was a Mr Harou. Conrad left Matadi with Harou and a convoy of thirty-one men.

p. 28   26. After thirty-five days Conrad reached Kinchassa, which was the registration port for the firm's Upper Congo fleet.

p. 29   27. On the trek Conrad had heard from a Mr Louette, who was escorting a sick agent of the Company back to Matadi, that one of the steamers had been wrecked and that all of them were disabled. It did not take months to repair the wrecked ship: five days after it had sunk it was brought back to Kinchassa. As a matter of fact, Conrad arrived at Kinchassa on August 2nd and left on August 3rd as second-in-command to Captain Koch, a Dane, who instructed him in the difficulties of Upper Congo navigation.

p. 29   28. The manager was a Mr Camille Delcommune, who had been aboard the wrecked ship, the *Florida*, when it went aground.

p. 30   29. Jack—a common word for sailor.

p. 33   30. The records of the Company show that a brickyard was in full function under a Mr Deligne.

p. 37   31. Mephistopheles—one of the seven chief devils in medieval demonology. Second of the fallen archangels to Satan.

p. 43   32. The Eldorado Exploring Expedition was really the Katanga Expedition under the manager's brother, Mr Alexandre Delcommune.

p. 48   33. Conrad's own ship would not be ready until the following June. Captain Koch fell ill, and Conrad took command of the *Roi des Belges* downstream for three days—the only fresh-water navigation he did.

p. 60   34. Conrad fell ill after the Congo trip. It was a long illness and a long convalescence, and it ended his career at sea. From this time he turned to writing.

p. 104 35. There is no record to show why Conrad decided to return to Belgium. In *A Personal Record* he speaks of going down with all his belongings from Kinchassa to Leopoldville, a trip on which he was almost drowned. He mentions being ill. It had been decided that he was not going to receive command of the *Florida*, which was given instead to a Captain Carlier (see 'An Outpost of Progress'). On October 19th Conrad decided to return home.

QUESTIONS

HEART OF DARKNESS

THESE questions are intended to take the student through a systematic study of the main features of the novel, and to help him to concentrate on working out a synthesis of the relevant facts that pertain especially to *one major aspect* of the work at a time. At the end of each section he should be able to conclude something reasonably concrete and responsible, whether he agrees with the drift of the questions or disputes their bias.

The questions in each group proceed systematically through the novel. Since most questions are prompted by a particular point on a particular page, the student should examine that point and then correlate it to other relevant parts of the novel. It is for this reason that such a comprehensive study should be undertaken only *after the first reading*. And although the particular page references for questions allow each to be referred to separately as a supplementary or occasional guide to independent study, nevertheless in each consecutively numbered group the later questions depend upon the premises established in the earlier ones, and thus to employ the full scope of the questions it is necessary to work sequentially through each group, and not to select items or questions as though they were separate or independent.

ESTABLISHING THE THEME

pp. 7–8 1. The Roman's reaction to the heart of darkness is described in seemingly contradictory terms: on the one side, 'incomprehensible', 'detestable', 'abomination', 'regrets', 'disgust', 'surrender', 'hate'; but, on the other side, 'fascination'. Relate these ambivalent feelings to Marlow's own experience of the heart of darkness.

p. 9 2. The heart of darkness seemed to 'throw a kind of light on me', Marlow says. Explain this ironic paradox.

p. 8 3. Contrast Marlow's 'idea' of empire with the Company's motives stated on page 16. Which view receives confirmation from his experiences in the Congo?

p. 16 4. Marlow's aunt thinks him 'a lower sort of apostle', 'an emissary of light'. What does Marlow think of her description of him?

pp. 18, 21 5. What is Marlow's first reaction to African natives? How does it compare with his attitude to the white man at that time? What feelings are beginning to seize Marlow in the statement 'I also was part of the great cause of these high and just proceedings'?

pp. 23–4 6. (*a*) Is there 'any idea at all connected with' the 'bit of white worsted' tied about the black man's neck? Relate this vestige of civilization to the description of the fireman and the helmsman on pages 53–4, 64–6, and 74.
(*b*) Compare this 'idea' of civilizing the natives with Marlow's initial glorious 'idea' of empire on page 8.

pp. 24–7 7. (*a*) Marlow respects the accountant's 'backbone' and achievements of character in keeping up appearances. But why does Marlow pause as he goes out of the accountant's office? What occurs to him?
(*b*) The groans of the dying interrupt the accountant's efficiency. Does the wilderness give this man any glimpse of himself and what he really is?

(*c*) Does Marlow respect the manager and the brick-maker, who 'keep up appearances'?

(*d*) What do you think is Marlow's ultimate regard for 'work', 'efficiency', 'backbone', and 'appear-ances'? Are they adequate forces of light in man to sustain him against the darkness? (See question 14.)

pp. 27–8   8. Examine the tone of Marlow's comment on the drunken white man's 'permanent improvement' to the non-existent road. Why does this follow direstly after a comparison of Christian bells to native drums? Does this tone persist in his description of the Central Station?

p. 35   9. Discuss the paradoxes in Kurtz's painting of the woman with the torch.

p. 38   10. Why does Marlow hate lies? Explain why he lies for Kurtz both to the brickmaker and to the Intended.

p. 43   11. Describe Marlow's reaction to the Eldorado Exploring Expedition. Has he any imperialist sympathies left for the 'idea', or the 'torch carriers'?

p. 49   12. Marlow, while going up the Congo to meet Kurtz, still feels that being kept busy with practical things to do hides the reality from one—hides the inner truth, 'luckily'.

(*a*) Why 'luckily'?

(*b*) What is the reality? Why does he feel the need to hide it?

(*c*) Compare his attitude (page 41) to what he thinks of the people busily doing things in Brussels when he returns (pages 104–5). What accounts for the change?

pp. 52–3   13. Marlow's kinship with the primitive jungle is de-veloped at this point. What does he begin to value above principles and possessions?

pp. 54–5   14. Marlow's instinctive regard for efficiency, work, and business-like order nevertheless remains, in spite of his affinity for the jungle. What article brings a tender response from him? Why? Select the phrase that represents the conflict between the call of the inhuman jungle and the call of civilization in him.

p. 56 15. What is Marlow's 'flash of insight'?

p. 58 16. Compare the response of the black men and the white men to the terrifying noise on the bank. Examine Marlow's tone to see which group he admires the more. Relate your answer here to your response to question 5.

pp. 60–1 17. Marlow introduces the moral idea of Restraint in speaking of the cannibals.
(*a*) What is the importance of restraint?
(*b*) Compare the cannibals' restraint to the manager's.
(*c*) Does Kurtz have any instinctive restraint?

pp. 69–71 18. As Charlie Marlow felt scorn for the man with the hole in his bucket trying to put out the fire, so he now feels scorn for his listeners. Why?

p. 72 19. Under the growing assault of the 'powers of darkness', Marlow separates three classes of human existence.
(*a*) What are they?
(*b*) Judge each character of the novel in relation to this classification.
(*c*) Justify your judgments from the text.

pp. 72–3 20. What two extremes of conviction are represented in Kurtz (*a*) by the report on the Suppression of Savage Customs, and (*b*) by the postscript to it?

p. 74 21. Immediately following the above reference, what is Marlow's estimate of 'civilization' and 'progress'? Is there still a lingering belief in the validity of 'doing something'? Note his references to the dead helmsman. (See question 14.)

pp. 81–6 22. The harlequin develops further the ambivalence of Kurtz's temperament. Trace the two sides of Kurtz's character from the harlequin's account of him. Which side predominates?

pp. 85–6 23. Marlow judges Kurtz from report. 'He was hollow at the core', he 'lacked restraint in the gratification of his various lusts'; 'there was something wanting in him', a 'deficiency'.

(*a*) By what standards are these condemnations made?

(*b*) Why does Marlow find uncomplicated savagery 'a positive relief', 'something that had a right to exist . . . in the sunshine'?

(*c*) How does the light imagery reinforce Marlow's judgment of Kurtz?

(*d*) Does Marlow change his opinions of Kurtz after meeting him?

p. 87 24. What is the phrase that most represents the image of Kurtz as Marlow looks at him for the first time?

p. 89 25. The gorgeous native woman is described as 'ominous and stately'. (She seems to be the 'soul' of this fecund, mysterious life.)

(*a*) Who else was described as 'stately and sinister'?

(*b*) Why does Conrad descriptively associate the two figures?

(*c*) How does this association reveal further the ambivalence in Kurtz's character referred to in question 23?

p. 90 26. The native threw up her arms as if to touch the sky. By this extending of her arms, relate her to another woman surrounded by shadows. Which 'soul' most claims Kurtz?

p. 91 27. Marlow is left with 'a choice of nightmares'. What two alternatives does he have? Which does he prefer? Why?

p. 92 28. Kurtz had ordered the attack on the steamer and then called it off. Why?

p. 93 29. What ironic factor is there in the description of the harlequin's pockets? Relate this ironic ambivalence to the central irony of the theme of the book so far.

p. 95   30. The climax of the novel is the direct confrontation between Kurtz and Marlow in the heart of darkness, not in the security of the steamer. Why was Marlow determined to make the confrontation alone? Why is he cocksure of himself?

p. 96   31. (*a*) What does Marlow mean when he says 'the foundations of our intimacy were being laid' at that moment?
(*b*) With what does he realize he is symbolically struggling?
(*c*) What terror does this struggle hold?

pp. 97–8 32. Kurtz had kicked himself free of restraint, of faith, of fear. His 'intelligence was clear'. He was under the spell of 'forgotten and brutal instincts', 'gratified and monstrous passions'. His soul had looked into itself and had gone mad. Marlow had the ordeal of looking into it too, of 'peeping over the edge'.
(*a*) Is Kurtz's the only soul Marlow is examining? What evidence is there that he is looking into a mirror?
(*b*) What was Kurtz's final burst of sincerity that withered one's belief in mankind (page 98)?
(*c*) Is Marlow's belief in mankind ever shaken? If so, is it ever restored?

p. 102   33. If Marlow's journey was really a journey into his own subconscious self, what is the significance of Kurtz's final words 'The horror! The horror!'? How was Kurtz's cry 'an affirmation', 'a moral victory' (page 104)?

pp. 103–4 34. When Marlow himself approached the edge of death, he had no pronouncement to make. Kurtz's dying face was 'the appalling face of a glimpsed truth', a truth which commingled desire and hate and yet was 'The horror!'.
  What is the truth that Marlow has glimpsed and remains loyal to? (Note that on page 108 he says the

stare was 'an immense stare embracing, condemning, loathing all the universe'.)

pp. 111– 114
35. When does Marlow feel the darkness to be triumphant and the light an illusion?

p. 114
36. Why does he protect the illusions of light in Kurtz's Intended with a lie? Refer back to your answer to question 10.

37. Is moral goodness only an illusion cherished by those who have never journeyed into the heart of darkness? Can one 'breathe dead hippo, so to speak, and not be contaminated' (page 72)?

38. Would Marlow's reaction to Kurtz have been different had he been surrounded by enlightened imperialism in the Congo? To what degree is Marlow's reaction to Kurtz conditioned by his disillusionment?

Assignment

Compose a complete and clear statement of the theme of the novel as it has been established by your study of the preceding questions. Be sure to account for all the factors (e.g. Marlow's changing moral position, his ideals and disillusionment, the dark truth glimpsed, the final interview) making certain that none contradicts your statement.

Now read carefully the following critical appraisal of *Heart of Darkness* by Florence H. Ridley (from 'The Ultimate Meaning of *Heart of Darkness*', 'Nineteenth-Century Fiction', June, 1963). Discuss the textual validity of this opposing point of view. Compile evidence from the novel to support it.

If all the parts of this tale be duly considered, they produce the ultimate comment that whatever the condition of a given civilization, its proponents are constantly threatened by the temptation to forsake its code, its ideals, whatever they may be, and thus become decivilized and in the process less than human. Only faith or devotion to something can provide the restraint necessary not to become like Kurtz. Only the preservation of her faith in Kurtz can protect the Belgian girl.

If there is irony in the fact that all Marlow has left is the Intended's faith in illusion, that 'her faith remained the only light', it was for Conrad the irony of the universal human condition. . . .

From such illusions alone comes light which can be opposed to the world's darkness.

This is why Conrad wrote to Wm. Blackwood 'The title I am thinking of is "The Heart of Darkness", but the narrative is not gloomy.' [1]

EXPLORING THE STRUCTURE

SETTING AND IMAGERY

pp. 3–4   1. The details of setting are mostly tranquil and serene. Where are ominous notes struck?

p. 4   2. Compare the phrase 'a benign immensity of unstained light' with the last sentence of the novel. Are these 'light' references an ironic frame for the narrative? Comment on the associations of 'unstained'.

pp. 3–6   3. What distinction is made between 'resemblance' and 'reality' in the opening paragraphs?

p. 5   4. Flashing through the first narrator's mind are thoughts of knights-errant's ships of history. What contrasting possibilities foreshadowing the story do their names evoke? (See note 4.)

p. 5   5. What predominating tone does the first narrator give to the history of commonwealth and empire—romantic idealism or ironic tragedy? Compare this

[1] © 1963 by The Regents of the University of California. Reprinted from NINETEENTH-CENTURY FICTION, Vol. XVIII, pp. 52–3, by permission of The Regents.

attitude with Marlow's developing view of imperialism as the tale proceeds.

p. 6   6. 'A brooding gloom in sunshine, a lurid glare under the stars.' What do these two degrees of light suggest? Why are these atmospheric tones in the first narrator's mind an appropriately sudden springboard from which to launch Marlow's tale?

NARRATOR LENS (*i.e. the point of view from which the novel is experienced*)

pp. 3–114 7. What does the device of having a first narrator allow Conrad to do with Marlow's story as it unfolds?

pp. 6, 9 8. (*a*) Select the phrases in which the first narrator estimates the typical Marlow narrative. What do they warn us of in our reactions to the story?
(*b*) Examine the Director of Companies' remark in the last paragraph of the novel as a concluding comment to Marlow's narrative. Compare this evidence of his character with his (i) checking the anchor's hold, and (ii) having left the sea.

pp. 39, 50, 9. On page 39 the first narrator's involvement in the
53, 69   story is contrasted with that of the other listeners. How does their mood remain the same and his begin to change? What is the significance of this technique of audience splitting?

pp. 4, 8, 10. The first narrator makes four important observations
114   on Marlow's sitting posture—two at the beginning, one in the middle (page 69), and one at the end. At the beginning Marlow seems to be 'preaching' and at the end 'meditating'. Explain the change from preaching to meditating. To what does the first narrator compare Marlow? Why? Look up the reference in an encyclopaedia and see note 11.

        11. Make a brief assessment of Marlow's character, noting his scope of intellect, eye for detail, capacity for sympathy, etc.

FURTHER STRUCTURAL PARALLELS AND CONTRASTS

p. 39 12. Conrad reportedly said to Edward Garnett, 'Before the Congo I was just a mere animal.' We live through the change that Conrad (Marlow) experienced. Is there any parallel change in the first narrator's experience (see page 39)? (Compare 'he was no more to us than a voice' with Marlow's comment on page 70.)

p. 39 13. If the first narrator's experience on hearing Marlow acts as a parallel to Marlow's experience on meeting Kurtz, whom do the other listeners parallel in Marlow's story? What do they have in common with the corresponding characters?

p. 8 14. Examine the paragraph on the Roman conquest of Britain for prefigurings of Marlow's journey into the heart of darkness. Note his impressions on page 43.

p. 3 15. (a) The first paragraph of the novel states that the 'flood had made' and that the yawl 'swung to her anchor'. In which direction is the yawl facing?
(b) The first narrator watches the back of the Director as he secures the anchor. Deduce where 'the offing' will be in relation to the narrator.
(c) Note the description of the offing and the water-way. Will the yawl 'swing to her anchor' again on the ebb?
(d) Examine the description of 'the offing' in the last paragraph of the novel. Is the offing in the same direction as in part (c) above?
(e) How does the light imagery of the opening and of the ending provide an appropriate parallel to the experience of the story?

pp. 3, 114 16. How do the descriptive comments of the first narrator at the beginning and the end of the novel achieve a change in focus from the particular to the universal? What does Conrad achieve by such a change in focus?

Do the parallel rivers emphasize or serve to counteract this change?

pp. 24–7, 17. (*a*) Discuss the accountant, the boilermaker, the
41–2, 55, harlequin, and the reference to Towson as similar
77–93 types of loyalty and devotion.

(*b*) Does the fact that their appearance or interests seem fantastic in the Congo invalidate their loyalty? Judge their characters in relation to those of the manager and his assistant, the brickmaker.

pp. 89–90, 18. Compare the women figures who represent the two
112, 35 sides of Kurtz's soul (see question 25 of Theme). Relate them to his painting.

pp. 69–71, 19. How do Marlow's audience resemble the people in
104–5 Brussels on his return?

pp. 108–9, 20. Compare the death imagery in the descriptions of (*a*)
12–14 the Intended's house at the end, and (*b*) the Company's offices at the beginning.

THE STRUCTURAL PROGRESSION OF THE NOVEL

p. 8 21. Marlow seems to admire the 'devotion to efficiency' in British imperialism. What is the other 'idea' that Marlow apparently believes in at the beginning? Trace the change in his comments on imperialism as the story proceeds.

p. 9 22. As factors of suspense, Marlow provides a forward glance at the climax and a mystery surrounding it.

(*a*) From his comments determine what the climax will be.

(*b*) To whom does he casually refer as 'the poor chap'?

(*c*) Evaluate Conrad's suspense technique in the rest of the novel.

p. 9 23. Marlow says 'It [the heart of darkness] was . . . the culminating point of my experience. It seemed to throw a kind of light on everything about me—*and into my thoughts.*' This statement implies that Marlow

is the hero of the story and that the nature of the
journey is symbolic.

(*a*) Where does Conrad intend to take us, using the
trip up the Congo as a symbolic journey?

(*b*) How do we know that Kurtz is not the hero of
the novel?

pp. 50, 69 24. Examine the moments of interruption in the narrative.
What do they serve to establish?

REVIEWING THE MYTHOLOGICAL
ACCOMPANIMENT TO MARLOW'S QUEST

BEGINNING THE JOURNEY

pp. 9–10   1. (*a*) Contrast Marlow's boyhood impression of Africa
with his present knowledge.

(*b*) What Christian condition does the phrase 'white
patch for a boy to dream . . . over' suggest?

(*c*) Why is it immediately followed by an image of
a snake?

(*d*) What overriding impression of the Congo are we
left with by the combination of darkness and snake?

p. 12   2. Why does the expedition start from a 'whited
sepulchre'? Where will a journey from a sepulchre
take us symbolically?

p. 14   3. Marlow's ushers are two women figures feverishly
'knitting black wool'. One walks toward him like a
somnambulist.

(*a*) What do they guard?

(*b*) Describe the atmosphere.

(*c*) Why does Marlow use the word 'piloted'?

(*d*) Why does he salute them with a Latin farewell?

(*e*) What mythological counterparts can you find for
these women?

pp. 12–16 4. Examine the details of the house. Why does Marlow
inject a note of grotesque comedy into the interview
with the doctor?

THE VOYAGE TO MATADI, THE COMPANY'S STATION

pp. 19–24 5. Marlow passes 'streams of death in life', and is piloted up the mouth of the big river by a Swede who tells him of a lost soul who hanged himself recently. Examine Marlow's description of his arrival at the Station in the light of the mythological journey symbolized.

p. 22 6. What two kinds of 'devils' drive the white man in the Congo? Which particular persons do they represent?

pp. 22–7 7. Comment on the references to 'Inferno' and the grove of death, to 'devils' and 'phantoms'.

THE CENTRAL STATION (KINCHASSA)

p. 28 8. Which devil of question 6 is running the Central Station?

p. 37 9. Who is the 'papier mâché Mephistopheles'? Why is he called that?

p. 38 10. What does Marlow say the narrative really is, just before he interrupts it?

THE JOURNEY TO THE INNER STATION

pp. 48–79 11. Is the underworld imagery continued in this section? Which level of the narrative takes precedence now— the literal or the symbolic?

p. 71 12. Kurtz is described as having literally taken a high seat over the devils of this land. What kind of figure does he become? What nouns are applied to him as this kind of figure?

pp. 95–8 13. The climax of the novel comes in the direct confrontation between Kurtz and Marlow in the heart of darkness, not in the security of the steamer. Note the details of setting for this climax. How are they appropriate to the underworld symbolism of the journey?

THE RETURN

pp. 98–9 14. The return from the heart of darkness begins with something like a ritual. What does Marlow call it? Why? What other descriptive details confirm his impression?

pp. 108–9 15. Why in the 'sepulchral city' are there death images in the description of the Intended's house and its interior? Why is the Intended bathed in a halo of light?

Assignment

In an essay of about 500–800 words, write a critical appreciation of the unifying factors in the structure of the novel. Take into account (*a*) parallels and contrasts, (*b*) unifying imagery, (*c*) details of setting, (*d*) the narrator point of view, (*e*) the suspense progression.

MINOR STUDIES

THE FARCICAL, FANTASTIC, GROTESQUE, AND MACABRE ELEMENTS

Examine briefly the instances below as examples of one or more of the following: comic relief, suspense, satire, irony, mystery, horror.

pp. 11–12 1. Fresleven's death at the hands of natives.

pp. 14–16 2. The interview with the doctor.

p. 18 3. Gran' Bassam, Little Popo, and the man-of-war shelling the bush.

pp. 21–2 4. The 'objectless blasting' at the Company's station and the vast artificial hole with no point to it.

pp. 22–4 5. The grove of death.

pp. 24–7 6. The Company's accountant.

pp. 27–8 7. The drunken white man keeping up the road.

p. 32 8. The hole in the pail.

Assignment

'The inclusion of the many fantastic elements undercuts the realism and endangers the credibility of the novel.' In a brief essay defend or refute this statement.

KURTZ'S CHARACTER

1. Compare and contrast the first three reports describing Kurtz, i.e. the accountant's, the manager's, and the brickmaker's. Do the reports begin to change at the beginning of Chapter II?

2. We hear of Kurtz's decision to return to the station. He abandons the return to go back to the heart of darkness. At this report Marlow 'seemed to see Kurtz for the first time'. What did he see? What does the incident reveal? Relate it (*a*) to Kurtz's leaving the steamer to return to the jungle rituals, and (*b*) to his ordering an attack on the steamer and calling it off.

3. There are 'strange rumours' about Kurtz, but there are also words of his quoted by the manager

to his uncle. What do these words reveal of Kurtz's character?

4. 'The wilderness . . . had taken him, loved him, embraced him, got into his veins, consumed his flesh, and sealed his soul to its own by the inconceivable ceremonies of some devilish initiation. He was its spoiled and pampered favourite.'

    (*a*) Examine Marlow's references to the wilderness and try to pin down the features of it that had become ingrained in the character of Kurtz.

    (*b*) Is our first sight of Kurtz an anti-climax?

5. How are the painting and the name 'Intended' both characteristic of Kurtz? Relate these to his postscript to the report on the Suppression of Savage Customs.

6. Compile a physical description of Kurtz from the novel.

7. Was Kurtz mad? Explain the heads on poles, the natives crawling to him, and the implication that he wished to be deified. How dangerous was he?

Assignment

Write a brief assessment of Conrad's use of graphic detail in the description of any three minor characters.

Compile complete character studies of Marlow and Kurtz from your responses to the previous questions on the novel.

AN OUTPOST OF PROGRESS

p. 117 1. Who is the narrator? Compare the advantages and restrictions of this narrator lens with the viewpoint in *Heart of Darkness*.

pp. 146–7 2. At the end of the story is the following sentence: 'The Managing Director of the Great Civilizing Company (since we know that civilization follows trade) landed first, and incontinently lost sight of the steamer.'

(a) What is the tone of this?

(b) Refer to other instances of this tone in the story.

(c) To what degree is this tone typical of Marlow's in *Heart of Darkness*?

(d) Since one story is told by Marlow and the other by an omniscient narrator (Conrad), to what extent is Marlow really an independent character?

p. 120 3. Read Conrad's description of Kayerts and Carlier between the following guide phrases: 'They were two perfectly insignificant and incapable individuals . . . the civilized nerves of the foolish and the wise alike.'

(a) Select phrases from pages 92 and 94 to support this description.

(b) Compare Kayerts and Carlier to the following characters in *Heart of Darkness*: (i) the Pilgrims, (ii) the listeners, (iii) the people in Brussels on Marlow's return.

(c) Does this paragraph reinforce or refute the theme of *Heart of Darkness*?

4. Discuss this story and *Heart of Darkness* as a condemnation of the imperialism of the 1890's.

pp. 131–2 5. Compare the description at the opening of Chapter II to the description of the cannibals in *Heart of Darkness*. What attitudes does Conrad force upon us concerning the tribal life of savages? Compare their 'regrets' with those of Kayerts and Carlier.

6. Examine the effects of isolation on the ethics of Kayerts and Carlier. Follow in detail their surrender.

7. Compare the details of setting in both this story and *Heart of Darkness*. In which does the setting have the more important role?

THE LAGOON

p. 167   1. Read the last paragraph carefully. List the features corresponding to passages in *Heart of Darkness*.

           2. Make a note on the framework of time in this story. Compare both the time frame and the setting to those of *Heart of Darkness*.

pp. 151-2   3. 'And the white man's canoe, advancing upstream in the short-lived disturbance of its own making, seemed to enter the portals of land from which the very memory of motion had forever departed.' Compare this description to that of the departure upstream from the Central Station in *Heart of Darkness*.

p. 157   4. Read the passage beginning 'The ever-ready suspicion of evil . . .' and continue to the end of the paragraph.
             (*a*) Relate the details of this passage, one by one, to the theme of *Heart of Darkness*.
             (*b*) Why does this reflection move from the word 'his' to 'our'?

           5. (*a*) Compare the compulsions and betrayals which characterize Arsat and Kurtz.
             (*b*) To what degree is the 'lady with the veiled face' a similar symbol of an ideal to the blindfolded woman in Kurtz's painting?

p. 159   6. 'There is a time when a man should forget loyalty and respect.'
             (*a*) Why is such an ominous note as this struck in what is apparently a tale of romance and dedication, of loyalty to and respect for love?
             (*b*) Which prevails in this story—the love for the brother or the love for the woman? What do the two loves symbolize?
             (*c*) The quoted statement suggests a time of commitment to something more important than 'loyalty and respect'. Does this commitment agree with the last sentence of the novel?

BROADER PROJECTS FOR ADVANCED STUDY

1. Examine the role of the narrator Marlow in the novels *Youth*, *Lord Jim*, and *Chance*. Does his character develop along with his narrative technique? Why is he not the central character in *Lord Jim* and *Chance*?

2. Compare *Heart of Darkness* to Robert Louis Stevenson's *The Beach of Falésa* or to William Golding's *Lord of the Flies*.

3. Study the relationship of the quest in *Heart of Darkness* to one of the following: Vergil's *Aeneid* (Book VI), Dante's *Divine Comedy* (Inferno), Milton's *Paradise Lost* (Books I and II).

4. Compare Marlow's return to Brussels with Gulliver's return to England in the last part (Book Four) of *Gulliver's Travels*.

5. Report on the symbolic use of the colours black and white in *Heart of Darkness*.

6. Give an account of British and Belgian imperialism in Africa. Refer to the careers of Cecil Rhodes, Livingstone, and Stanley. Is Conrad's picture in *Heart of Darkness* and *An Outpost of Progress* a fair one?

7. Read T. S. Eliot's 'The Hollow Men' and relate its theme to that of *Heart of Darkness*. Is the art of *Heart of Darkness* a good working example of Eliot's idea of the 'objective correlative'?

8. Discuss the several kinds of irony to be found in *Heart of Darkness*.

9. Is Conrad a second Kipling?

10. Relate Leggatt of *The Secret Sharer* and Kurtz as examples of Conrad's *alter ego*.

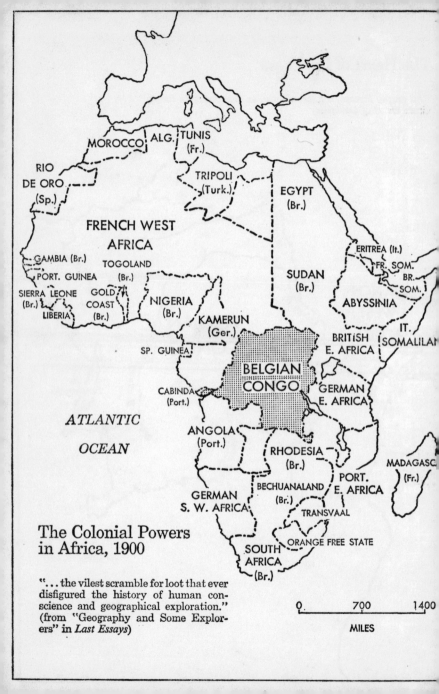

The Colonial Powers
in Africa, 1900

"... the vilest scramble for loot that ever disfigured the history of human conscience and geographical exploration." (from "Geography and Some Explorers" in *Last Essays*)